Hila mings
From
Grandma
1949
39

P9-CEZ-859

HEIDI

By
JOHANNA SPYRI

Illustrated by
ARTHUR JAMESON

★

WHITMAN PUBLISHING CO.
RACINE, WISCONSIN

Copyright, 1944, by
WHITMAN PUBLISHING COMPANY
RACINE, WISCONSIN
Printed in U.S.A.

Contents

Part I

Part II

A Tall, Sturdy-looking Girl Led a Small
Child up the Steep Mountain Path

Chapter 1

THE ALM-UNCLE

From the pleasantly situated old town of Mayenfeld a footpath leads up through shady green meadows to the foot of the mountains. Any one who follows it will soon catch the pungent fragrance of grassy pasture lands, for the footpath goes up straight and steep to the Alps.

One bright, sunny June morning, a tall, sturdy-looking girl, evidently a native of the mountains, was seen climbing this narrow path. She led by the hand a little girl, whose cheeks glowed as if there were a flame under her dark skin. And what wonder? In spite of the hot June sun, the child was bundled up as if for protection against the keenest cold. She could not have been five years old, but it was impossible to tell anything about her natural figure, for she wore two or three dresses, one over the other, and a big red cotton handkerchief around her neck. Her feet seemed lost in heavy hobnailed shoes as she made her hot and laborious way up the mountain.

At the end of an hour of steady climbing the two girls came to the hamlet that lies halfway up the Alm and is called *Im Dörfli,* or the Little Village. Here they were greeted by nearly everyone they met, for the older girl had reached her childhood home. However she did not pause, but hurried on, answering all questions and returning greetings as she walked. As she was passing the last of the scattered cottages, a voice from the doorway cried:

"Wait a moment, Dete, I'll go with you, if you are bound up the mountain."

The big girl stopped; immediately the child withdrew her hand and sat down on the ground.

"Are you tired, Heidi?" asked her companion.

"No, I am hot," replied the little girl.

"We are almost there," said her companion, encouragingly.

Just then a large, pleasant-looking woman came out of the cottage. The little girl jumped to her feet and followed the two women up the mountain.

"Really, Dete, where are you taking the child?" asked the newcomer. "It is your sister's little girl, isn't it—the orphan?"

"Yes, it is," replied the other. "I am taking her up to her grandfather; she will have to stay there."

"What! The little girl is going to live with the Alm-Uncle? You must have lost your senses, Dete! The old man will send you back with such a scheme as that."

"He can't; he's her grandfather, and it is time for him to look out for her. I have had her till now, Barbel, but I have had a good position offered me in Frankfurt. I can't take the child, and her grandfather must do his part."

"That's very well, if he were like other men," replied the portly Barbel with indignation. "But you know what he is. He will have nothing to do with a living soul. He never sets foot in a church; and if once in a twelve-month he comes down with his thick staff, everyone keeps out of his way and is afraid of him. What will he do with a child—especially with such a young one?"

"Nevertheless," said Dete stubbornly, "he's her grandfather, and it's his business to look after her. He won't do her any harm; if he does, he will have to answer for it, not I."

"I should like to know," said Barbel insinuatingly, "what the old man has on his conscience that makes him look so fierce and live all alone up there on the Alm and keep almost hidden from sight. People tell all sorts of stories about him. Of course you know something about it, Dete. Your sister must have told you; didn't she?"

"Of course she did, but I hold my tongue. If he should hear of it, I should suffer!"

Barbel had long desired to know the real cause of the Alm-Uncle's peculiarities, but she had only recently married into the village. Before that her home had been down in the valley at Prättigau. Her friend, Dete, on the contrary, had lived in Dörfli until a year ago. Then her mother had died and she had gone down to Ragatz, where the Baths are, and had found a position as chambermaid in a hotel. She had come from Ragatz that very morning with the little girl, having had the chance to ride as far as Mayenfeld on a hay wagon which an acquaintance of hers was driving home.

Barbel thought that this was a good chance to find out something. She seized Dete's arm confidentially and said:

"One can learn the real truth from you instead of the gossip which is talked. Come now, tell me what is the matter with the old man? Has he always been so feared? Has he always been such a hermit?"

"I can't tell whether he has always been so or not. I am twenty-six now, and he is certainly seventy, and of course I never saw him when he was young. If I were certain that he would never again be seen in Prättigau, I might tell you all sorts of things about him; my mother was from Domleschg, and so was he."

"There now, Dete, what do you mean?" exclaimed Barbel, a little offended. "You need not be so severe on our gossip in Prätti-gau. Besides, I can keep a secret or two if need be. Tell me; you shan't regret it."

"Well then, I will; but mind you hold your tongue," said Dete warningly. She glanced around to see if Heidi was close enough to hear, but the child was not to be seen. She must have ceased following them some distance back, but in their lively conversation they had not noticed it.

"There she is," exclaimed Barbel, pointing to a place quite distant from the path. "She is climbing up the cliffs with the goatherd Peter and his goats. Why is he so late today with his animals? But it is just as well, for he can look after the child, and you will be all the better able to talk with me."

"Peter needn't trouble himself to look after her," said Dete. "She is not dull for a child of five years. She keeps her eyes open, and it's a good thing for her that she does. The old man has nothing to leave her but his two goats and his mountain hut."

"And did he once have more?" asked Barbel.

"He? Well, I should say that he did once have more," replied Dete warmly. "He used to have the finest farm in Domleschg, but he drank and gambled away the whole property. His father and mother died, first one and then the other, from sheer grief. Then the son disappeared, leaving nothing behind him but a bad name. It was reported that he had gone with the soldiers to Naples, and nothing more was heard of him for twelve or fifteen years.

"Then he suddenly appeared again in Domleschg with a half-grown boy. Every door was closed to him, and this made him very bitter. He said he would never set foot in Domleschg again, and he came here to Dörfli. He had married while he was away, but his wife had died; so he and his son lived alone. He must have had some money still, for he let the boy Tobias learn the carpenter's trade. Tobias was a steady fellow and well thought of by all the people in Dörfli.

"But nobody had confidence in the old man. It was said that he had gotten into trouble in Naples, that he had killed somebody in a quarrel. But we recognize the relationship, for my mother's grandmother was his grandmother's first cousin. So we called him

Uncle, and as we are related to almost all the people in Dörfli, on father's side, they all call him Uncle. Ever since he went up on the Alm he has been known as the Alm-Uncle."

"But what became of Tobias?" asked Barbel eagerly.

"He married my sister, Adelheid," said Dete. "They were very happy together, but it didn't last long. Two years later, while Tobias was working on a new house, a beam fell on him and killed him. Adelheid's grief threw her into a violent fever, from which she did not recover. She never was very strong, and was often in such a condition that it was almost impossible to tell whether she was asleep or awake. Only two weeks after Tobias's death Adelheid too was buried.

"People said it was a judgment on the uncle for his godless life. It was even said so to his face, and he grew more surly than ever. He no longer spoke to anyone, and everyone avoided him.

"Suddenly it was reported that he had gone up on the Alm, and there he has stayed ever since.

"Mother and I took Adelheid's little child; she was a year old. Last summer mother died, and as I wanted to work down at the Baths, I took her to board with old Ursel up in Pfäfferserdorf. I stayed at the Baths all winter, but now the lady I worked for wants to take me home with her to Frankfurt. We start day after tomorrow. It's a good place, I tell you."

"And are you going to give the child to the old man up there? I'm surprised that you should think of such a thing, Dete," said Barbel reproachfully.

"I have done my duty," Dete retorted. "I can't take a child scarcely five years old to Frankfurt. But where are you going, Barbel? We are halfway up the Alm now."

"I have reached the place where I was going. I want to speak to old goatherd Peter's wife. She does spinning for me in winter. So good-by, Dete; good luck to you!"

Dete shook her companion's hand and stood still while Barbel went into the dilapidated little dark-brown mountain hut in a hollow, where it was somewhat sheltered from the wind. Here dwelt the goatherd Peter, the eleven-year-old boy who every morning went down to Dörfli to get the goats and drive them up on the Alm, to feed till evening on the short, nourishing herbs. Then Peter would hurry down again with the light-footed animals, give a shrill whistle through his fingers as soon as he reached Dörfli, and all the owners would immediately come and get their goats. Little boys and girls came for the most part, for the creatures were peaceful and harmless. All through the summer it was the only time in the day when Peter associated with his fellow-beings; the rest of the time he lived alone with his goats.

To be sure, he had his mother and blind grandmother at home; but he had to go away very early in the morning, and come back from Dörfli late in the evening. So in order to play with the children as long as possible, he spent only enough time at home to swallow his bread and milk.

His father, who had also been called Peter the goatherd, because he had followed the same calling, had met with an accident some years before while felling trees. His mother, whose real name was Brigitte, was still called "goatherd Peter's wife," and the blind grandmother was known, by old and young, simply by the name of Grandmother.

Dete looked around for the children with the goats. But as they were nowhere in sight, she climbed a little higher, where she could have a better view of the Alm down to the foot. She peered first this way, then that, growing more and more impatient when she could not see them.

Meanwhile the children were coming by a roundabout way. Peter knew many spots where there were good shrubs and bushes for his goats to nibble; so he frequently wandered from the path

with his flock. At first Heidi in her heavy garb climbed after them, panting with heat and discomfort. She looked at Peter, who jumped about without any difficulty in his bare feet and light trousers, then at the goats with their small, slender legs climbing still more easily over bushes and stones and steep crags.

Suddenly she sat down on the ground and pulled off her shoes and stockings. She stood up again, took off her thick, red neckerchief, unfastened her Sunday frock, quickly took that off, and began to unhook her everyday dress. This she had worn under the other, to save her Aunt Dete the trouble of carrying it. Quick as lightning came off also the everyday frock, and there the child stood in her light underclothes, stretching her bare arms out of her short chemise sleeves. She laid her clothes in a neat little pile on the ground and hurried up the mountain, jumping and climbing after the goats as easily as Peter did.

When she came running after him in her new costume, a grin spread over his face. He looked back and saw the little pile of clothes, and the grin grew still broader.

Heidi, feeling free and light, began to talk. She had all sorts of questions to ask Peter. How many goats did he have? Where was he going with them? What would he do when he reached there? Finally the children with the goats approached the hut and came in sight of Aunt Dete.

"Heidi," she screamed, "what have you been doing? What is the matter with you? Where are your dresses and your neckerchief? Where are your brand-new shoes and the stockings I made you?"

The child calmly pointed down the mountain and said; "There!"

The aunt followed the direction of her finger. "You careless girl!" she cried. "Why did you take everything off?"

"I didn't need them," said Heidi, not looking in the least sorry for what she had done.

"Oh, you careless, senseless Heidi!" the aunt went on, lamenting and scolding. "It will take half an hour for anyone to go down there again! Peter, run back and get the things! Be quick; don't stand there staring at me as if you were nailed to the ground."

"I am late already," said Peter slowly.

Dete looked at him impatiently. "Come here! Do you see this?" She held up a new five-centime piece, which glistened in the sunlight.

Peter looked at it. Then suddenly he turned and raced down the Alm, not stopping until he reached the little pile of clothes. He picked them up and brought them back so quickly that Dete gave him his money without delay. Peter put it in his pocket, and his face lighted with a broad grin, for such a treasure did not often fall to his share.

"You may carry the things on up to the uncle's, as long as you're going that way," continued Aunt Dete, while she set about climbing the steep cliff, which rose behind Peter's hut. The boy willingly undertook the task and followed, carrying the bundle in his left hand, and swinging his stick in his right. Heidi and the goats skipped and jumped along merrily by his side.

In about three quarters of an hour the procession reached the height where, on a jutting cliff, stood the old uncle's hut, with a view of the valley below. Behind the hut stood three ancient fir trees with long, thick, untrimmed branches. Farther back, the mountain rose higher still, with its lovely, fertile pastures, and surmounted with bare, steep cliffs.

The uncle had made himself a seat by the side of the hut looking down into the valley. Here he sat with his pipe in his mouth, his hands resting on his knees, calmly watching the children, Aunt Dete, and the goats. Aunt Dete had gradually been left behind, and Heidi was the first to reach the hut. She went straight to the old man and held out her hand.

"How do you do, grandfather?" she said.

"Well, well, what does this mean?" asked the old man roughly, giving her a long, penetrating look from under his bushy eyebrows. Heidi gazed back at him in surprise. She had never seen anyone like her grandfather, with his long beard and heavy gray eyebrows meeting in the middle of his forehead like a thicket. In the meantime Dete had arrived with Peter, who waited expectantly to see what would happen.

"I wish you good morning, uncle," said Dete. "I have brought Tobias and Adelheid's child to you. You will hardly know her, for you haven't seen her since she was a year old."

"Well, what can the child do here with me?" asked the old man curtly. Then he turned to Peter. "You there! Go along with your goats. You are none too early. Take mine too!"

Peter obeyed without delay and disappeared, for the uncle had made it plain that he was not wanted.

"Heidi must stay with you, uncle," said Dete. "I am sure I have done my duty by her these four years, and now it is your turn to do what you can for her."

"Indeed?" said the old man, and his eyes flashed. "Suppose the child begins to fret and whine for you; what shall I do with her then?"

"That is your business," retorted Dete. "I am sure no one told me what to do with the little one when she was given into my hands, only a year old, and I already had enough to do to take care of myself and mother. Now I must look out for myself, and you are next of kin to the child. If you can't have her, do what you please with her. You will have to answer for her, if she comes to any harm. You don't want to have anything more laid to your charge."

Dete's conscience was not quite easy; she became excited and said more than she had intended. The uncle rose at her last words. He gave her such a look that she took several steps backward. Then he stretched out his arm and said imperatively:

"Get you gone down where you came from, and don't show yourself here again very soon!"

Dete did not need to be told twice.

"Good-by, then; and good-by to you too, Heidi," she said quickly and hurried down the mountain to Dörfli. She was quite disgusted when nearly everyone she met stopped her to ask about the child.

"What? You left her with the Alm-Uncle?" "How could you do so?" "The poor little soul!" were the exclamations she heard on every side.

Dete pushed on as fast as she could go, and was glad to leave the village behind her. She did not feel quite easy in her own conscience, for the dying mother had given the child to her. But she quieted her misgivings by telling herself that she would soon be earning a great deal of money and could do something again for Heidi.

Chapter 2

AT THE GRANDFATHER'S

~~~~~~

AFTER DETE had disappeared, the uncle sat down again on the bench and blew great clouds of smoke from his pipe, while he kept his eyes fixed on the ground without saying a word. Meanwhile Heidi was content to look about her. She discovered the goats' shed near the hut and peeped into it. It was empty.

The child continued her investigations and came to the fir trees behind the hut. The wind was blowing hard, and it whistled and roared through the branches. Heidi stood still and listened. When it subsided somewhat she went around to the other side of the hut and came back to her grandfather. She placed herself in front of him, put her hands behind her, and gazed at him. Her grandfather looked up.

"What do you want to do?" he asked as she continued standing in front of him without moving.

"I want to see what you have in the hut," said Heidi.

"Come along, then!" The grandfather got up and started toward the hut. "Bring your bundle of clothes."

"I shan't want them any more," said Heidi.

The old man looked sharply at the child, whose black eyes shone in expectation. "She's not lacking in intelligence," he thought. Then he said aloud, "Why won't you need them any more?"

"I'd rather go like the goats, with their swift little legs."

"So you shall, but bring the things along," commanded the grandfather. "They can be put in the cupboard."

Heidi obeyed. The old man opened the door, and Heidi followed him into the one-room hut. In it were a table and a chair. In one corner was the grandfather's bed, in another the fireplace where hung the large kettle. On the other side, in the wall, was a large door, which the grandfather opened; it was the cupboard. There hung his clothes, and on one shelf lay his shirts, stockings, and linen. On another were plates, cups, and glasses and, on the top shelf, a loaf of bread, smoked meat, and cheese. Everything the Alm-Uncle owned and needed was kept in this closet. As soon as he had opened the door, Heidi came running with her bundle and pushed it in, as far back of her grandfather's clothes as possible. Then she looked carefully around the room.

"Where shall I sleep, grandfather?" she asked.

"Wherever you wish," he replied.

This was to Heidi's liking. She looked into every nook and corner to find the best place to sleep. In the corner by her grandfather's bed stood a little ladder, which led to the hayloft. Heidi climbed this. There lay a fresh, fragrant heap of hay, and through a round window one could look far down into the valley.

"I will sleep here," Heidi called down. "It is lovely! Just come and see how lovely it is here, grandfather!"

"I know all about it," sounded from below.

"I am going to make a bed," called the child again as she ran busily to and fro in the loft. "But you must bring me a sheet, for the bed must have a sheet for me to sleep on."

"Well, well," said the grandfather below.

After a few moments he went to the cupboard and found a long, coarse piece of cloth, which might serve for a sheet. When he came up the ladder, Heidi had made a neat little bed in the hayloft, with the hay piled up higher at one end to form the head.

"That is made very nicely," said the grandfather; "but wait a moment." He took up a big armful of hay and made the bed as thick again, in order that the hard floor might not be felt through it. "Now we'll put on the sheet."

With Heidi's help he spread the sheet over the hay, and where it was too broad or too long Heidi quickly tucked it under. Now it appeared quite trim and neat, and Heidi stood looking at it thoughtfully.

"We have forgotten one thing, grandfather," she said.

"What is that?" he asked.

"The coverlet. When we go to bed we creep in between the sheet and the coverlet."

"Is that so? But suppose I haven't any?" asked the old man.

"Oh, then it's no matter," said Heidi soothingly. "We can take more hay for a coverlet." She was about to run to the haymow again, but her grandfather stopped her.

"Wait a moment," he said, and went down the ladder to his own bed. When he came back, he laid a large, heavy linen bag on the floor.

"Isn't that better than hay?" he asked. Heidi pulled at the bag with all her might and main, trying to unfold it, but her little hands could not manage the heavy thing. Her grandfather helped, and when it was finally spread out on the bed, it looked very neat and comfortable.

"That is a splendid coverlet," said Heidi admiringly. "The whole bed is lovely! How I wish it were night so that I could lie down in it!"

"I think we might have something to eat first," said the grandfather. "What do you say?"

In her happiness over the bed, Heidi had forgotten everything else, but now she realized she was hungry. She had had nothing all day except a piece of bread and a cup of weak coffee early in the morning before she began her long journey.

"Yes, I think so too," she said eagerly.

"Well, let us go down," said the old man and followed close upon the child's steps. He went to the fireplace, pushed the large kettle aside and drew forward the little one that hung on the chain. He sat down on the three-legged wooden stool and kindled a fire. When the kettle began to boil, he put a big piece of cheese on a long iron fork. He moved it this way and that, until it was a golden yellow on all sides.

Heidi looked on with eagerness. Suddenly she jumped up and ran to the cupboard, and kept going back and forth. When the grandfather brought the toasted cheese to the table, it was already nicely laid with the round loaf of bread, two plates and two knives, for Heidi had noticed everything in the cupboard and knew that all would be needed for the meal.

"That is right, to think of doing something yourself," said the grandfather, laying the cheese on the bread and putting the tea-pot on the table. "But there is something still lacking."

Heidi saw how invitingly the steam came out of the pot and ran quickly to the cupboard. There was only one little bowl there, but behind it stood two glasses. The child came back with the bowl and glasses and placed them on the table.

"Very good. You know how to help yourself, but where are you going to sit?"

The grandfather himself was sitting in the only chair. Heidi ran to the fireplace, brought back the little three-legged stool and sat down on it.

"Well, you have a seat, only it is rather low," said the grandfather. "Even in my chair you would be too short to reach the table; but wait—"

He rose, filled the little bowl with milk, placed it on the chair, and pushed it close to the three-legged stool, so that Heidi had a table in front of her. The grandfather laid a large slice of bread and a piece of the golden cheese on the chair and said:

"Now eat!"

He seated himself on the corner of the table and began his dinner. Heidi grasped her bowl and drank and drank without stopping, for she was very thirsty after her long journey. Then she drew a long breath and set down the bowl.

"Do you like the milk?" asked her grandfather.

"I never tasted such good milk before," answered Heidi eagerly.

"Then you must have some more!" The grandfather filled the bowl again to the brim and placed it before her. He spread her bread with toasted cheese as soft as butter. It tasted delicious, with frequent drinks of milk.

When the meal was over, the grandfather went out to the goat-shed to put it in order. Heidi watched as he swept it with a broom and laid down fresh straw for the animals to sleep on. Then he went to his little shop, cut some round sticks, shaped a board, made some holes in it, put the round sticks into them; and suddenly it was a stool like his own, only much higher. Heidi was speechless with amazement.

"What is this, Heidi?" he asked.

"It is a stool for me, because it is so high. You made it all at once," said the astonished child.

"She knows what she sees; her eyes are in the right place," remarked the grandfather to himself.

Evening was coming on. A mighty wind had sprung up and was whistling and moaning through the fir trees. It sounded so beautiful in Heidi's ears that she was delighted, and skipped and jumped under the firs as if she were experiencing the greatest pleasure of her life. The grandfather stood in the doorway and watched the child.

A shrill whistle sounded. Down from above came goat after goat, leaping like a hunting train, with Peter in the midst of them.

With a shout of joy Heidi rushed in among the flock and greeted her old friends of the morning, one after the other.

When they reached the hut, they all stood still, and two lovely slender goats—one white, the other brown—left the flock to rush up to the grandfather. He stood waiting, as he did every evening, holding some salt in his hands, and they licked his fingers eagerly. Peter disappeared with the rest of his flock.

"Are these both ours, grandfather?" asked Heidi, stroking first one goat and than the other, for she was delighted with the little creatures. "Will they go into the shed? Will they stay with us always?"

"Yes," said the grandfather. "Now go and bring out your bowl and bread."

Heidi obeyed and came back at once. The grandfather milked the goat and filled the bowl and cut off a piece of bread. "Now eat your supper," he told her, "and then go up to bed! Your Aunt Dete left a bundle for you; your nightgowns and other things are in it. You will find it downstairs in the closet. I must attend to the goats now; so sleep well!"

"Good night, grandfather—what are the goats' names, grandfather?" asked the child, running after the old man and the goats as they disappeared in the shed.

"The white one is named Schwänli (little swan), and the brown one, Bärli (little bear)," answered the grandfather.

"Good night, Schwänli! Good night, Bärli!" called Heidi. Then she sat down on the bench and ate her bread and drank her milk; but the strong wind almost blew her off from her seat. So she finished hastily, went in and climbed up to her bed, where she slept as soundly as a princess in a beautiful, carved bed of some precious wood.

Not long after, even before it was wholly dark, the grandfather also went to bed. In the night the wind blew with such force that its blasts made the whole hut tremble, and every rafter creak. It howled and groaned down the chimney like voices in distress, and outside in the fir trees it raged with such fury that now and then a bough was broken off.

In the middle of the night the grandfather rose and said to himself:

"She may be afraid."

He climbed the ladder and went to Heidi's bedside. The moon

shone through the round opening and fell directly on Heidi's couch. She lay with one rosy cheek pillowed on her little round arm. She must have been dreaming happy dreams, for there was a look of contentment on her face. The grandfather gazed down at the sweetly sleeping child until the moon went behind a cloud and it was dark. Then he went back to bed.

Chapter 3

IN THE PASTURE

HEIDI WAS awakened early in the morning by a loud whistle. When she opened her eyes, a flood of sunshine was pouring through the round window on her bed and on the hay close by, so that everything about shone like gold. Heidi looked around her in amazement and did not know where she was.

Then she heard her grandfather's deep voice outside, and everything came back to her. She jumped out of bed, dressed quickly, climbed down the ladder and ran out in front of the hut. There stood goatherd Peter with his flock, and the grandfather was bringing Schwänli and Bärli out of the shed to join the other goats.

"Would you like to go to the pasture, too?" asked the grandfather. Heidi was pleased and jumped up and down for joy.

"Then wash your face, or the sun will laugh at you when it is shining so brightly up there and sees that you are dirty. See, everything is ready!"

The grandfather pointed to a tub of water standing before the door in the sunshine. Heidi ran to it and splashed and rubbed until she was all shining. Meanwhile the grandfather went into the hut and called Peter:

"Come here, general of the goats, and bring your haversack with you."

Peter obeyed, bringing the little bag in which he carried his meager dinner.

"Open it," said the old man; and he put in a large piece of bread

28

and an equally large piece of cheese. Peter opened his round eyes wide in amazement, for both pieces were half as large again as what he had brought for his own dinner.

"Now in goes the little bowl," continued the uncle, "for the child cannot drink the way you do, right from the goat; she doesn't know how. Milk two bowlfuls at noon for her, as she is to go with you and stay until you come down again. Take care that she doesn't fall over the rocks, do you hear?"

Heidi came running in.

"Can the sun laugh at me now, grandfather?" she asked eagerly. She had rubbed her face, neck, and arms so vigorously with the coarse towel, which her grandfather had hung by the water tub, that she looked as red as a lobster. Her grandfather smiled.

"No; now he has nothing to laugh at," he admitted. "But to-night, when you come home, you must go in all over, like a fish, for after running about like the goats you will have black feet. Now you can march along."

So she went merrily up the Alm. The sky was a deep blue, and the sun shone on the green mountain. Everywhere there were flowers: delicate primroses and great patches of blue gentians and golden rock-roses nodding in the sunshine. Heidi was so charmed she almost forgot Peter and the goats. She ran far ahead and then off to one side, for the ground shone red here and yellow there and enticed her in every direction. Wherever she went she plucked quantities of the flowers and put them in her apron. She wanted to carry them all home and put them into the hay in her sleeping room, that it might look as it did here.

Peter had a hard time keeping her in sight, and the goats were as bad as Heidi. They ran hither and thither, and he was obliged to whistle and shout and swing his rod continually in order to drive all the stragglers together.

"Where have you gone now. Heidi?" he called almost angrily.

"Here," sounded from some indefinite place. Peter could see no one, for Heidi was sitting on the ground behind a knoll, which was thickly covered with fragrant wild flowers. The whole air around was filled with the sweet odor, and Heidi had never breathed anything so exquisite before. She sat down among the flowers and drew in long breaths of the perfume.

"Come along!" called Peter again. "You must not fall down over the cliffs; the uncle charged me not to let you."

"Where are the cliffs?" asked Heidi.

"Up there, 'way up. We still have a long way to go; so come along now! Up at the very top sits the old robber-bird croaking."

Heidi jumped up and ran to Peter with her apron full of flowers.

"You have enough flowers already," he said. "If you pick them all now, there won't be any left for tomorrow."

The last reason convinced Heidi; and she went along with Peter. The goats also behaved better and hurried along, for they smelled the good herbage in the distance on the high pasture land.

The pasture where Peter usually went with his goats lay at the foot of the high cliff. The lower part was covered with bushes and fir trees, but toward the top it was quite bald and steep. On one side of the mountain there were deep chasms. The grandfather was quite right in warning Peter about them.

When Peter reached this spot on the heights, he took off his bag and laid it carefully in a little hollow in the ground. He knew that the wind often rushed across in strong gusts, and he did not wish to see his precious possessions roll down the mountain. Then he stretched himself out on the sunny ground to rest from the exertion of climbing.

In the meantime Heidi had taken off her apron, rolled it up tightly with the flowers inside, and laid it close to the lunch bag. Then she sat down beside Peter and looked around. The valley lay far below in the morning sunshine. In front of her she saw a great wide field of snow, stretching high up into the deep blue sky. On the left stood an enormous mass of rock, on each side of which rose a higher tower of bald, jagged crags and looked sternly down. Heidi sat quite still, drinking in the sunlight, the fresh air, and the delicate fragrance of the flowers. She wanted nothing more than to remain here forever.

Then she heard above her a loud, shrill screaming and croaking. The largest bird she had ever seen was flying in wide circles on outstretched wings.

"Peter! Peter! Wake up!" cried Heidi at the top of her voice. "See, there is the robber-bird! See! See!"

Peter jumped up and looked at the bird which was flying higher and higher until finally it disappeared over the gray cliffs.

"Where has he gone?" asked Heidi.

"Home to his nest," was Peter's answer.

"Is his home 'way up there? Oh, how lovely to be so high up! Why does he scream so?" asked Heidi again.

"Because he can't help it."

"Let us climb up there and see where his home is," Heidi suggested.

"No! No! No!" Peter burst out in disapproval. "Even a goat can't climb up there, and the uncle said you must not fall over the cliff."

Then Peter suddenly began such a whistling and calling that Heidi did not know what was going to happen. But the goats must have understood the sound, for one after another they came jumping down until the whole flock was grazing on the green slope, or amusing themselves by butting one another with their horns. Heidi laughed and jumped up and ran around among the goats as they played together. Each of the little creatures had a distinct individuality of its own, and she wanted to make the personal acquaintance of each one.

Meanwhile Peter had brought out the bag and arranged the four pieces of bread and cheese on the ground in a square, the larger pieces on Heidi's side, the smaller ones on his side. He took the little bowl and milked sweet, fresh milk from Schwänli into it and placed it in the middle of the square. Then he called Heidi, but he had to call longer for her than for the goats. She had become so interested in the antics of her new playmates that she could think of nothing else.

But Peter knew how to make himself understood. He called till he made the rocks above echo, and Heidi appeared. The table he had laid looked so inviting that she danced around it for joy.

"Stop jumping; it is time to eat," said Peter. "Sit down and begin."

Heidi sat down.

"Is the milk mine?" she asked, contemplating with satisfaction the neat square and the bowl in the middle.

"Yes," answered Peter, "and the two large pieces of bread and cheese are yours, too. When you have drunk all the milk, you can have another bowlful from Schwänli. Then it is my turn."

"And where will you get your milk?" Heidi wanted to know.

"From my goat—from Schnecke. Now eat!" commanded Peter once more.

Heidi began with her milk, and as soon as she set down her empty bowl Peter rose and filled it again. Heidi broke some of her bread into it and gave the rest to Peter. She also gave him her portion of cheese.

"You may have that. I have enough," she said.

Peter looked at Heidi in speechless amazement, for never in his life had he been able to say he had enough. He hesitated, for he could not really believe that Heidi was in earnest. She persisted in offering the bread and cheese, and when he did not take it,

she laid it on his knee. Then he saw that she meant it for him, seized the prize, nodded his thanks, and made the most satisfactory dinner of his life. Meantime Heidi watched the goats.

"What are their names, Peter?" she asked.

He knew them all well enough and could keep them in his head all the better because he had little else to store away there. So he began and without hesitation named one after the other, pointing to each one as he did so.

There was the big Türk with his powerful horns. He was always trying to butt all the others, and if he came near, most of them ran away and would have nothing to do with their rough comrade. The brave Distelfinck, a slender, nimble little goat, was the only one that did not avoid him, but often ran at him so swiftly and skilfully that the big Türk would stand still in astonishment and make no further attack.

There was the little white Schneehöpli, who suddenly began bleating so beseechingly, that Heidi ran to her and put her arms around her neck.

"What is the matter, Schneehöpli? Why do you cry so?" she asked sympathetically.

The goat pressed close to Heidi's side and became quiet.

Peter called out from where he was sitting, with frequent interruptions while he took a bite and a swallow:

"She does so because the old one doesn't come with her any more. They sold her and sent her to Mayenfeld day before yesterday."

"Who is the old one?" asked Heidi.

"Why, the mother, of course," was the reply.

"Where is the grandmother?" asked Heidi again.

"Hasn't any."

"And the grandfather?"

"Hasn't any."

"You poor Schneehöpli," said Heidi, drawing the little creature close. "Don't cry any more. I will come with you every day, and you won't be alone."

Schneehöpli rubbed her head contentedly against Heidi's shoulder and bleated no more.

The animals began to climb up to the bushes again. Heidi stood watching them, her hands behind her back.

"Peter," she said, "the prettiest of them all are Schwänli and Bärli."

"Of course they are," was the reply. "The Alm-Uncle brushes and washes them and gives them salt, and he has the best shed."

Suddenly Peter jumped up and leaped after the goats. Heidi

ran after him; she felt that something must have happened. Peter ran through the midst of the flock to the side of a steep precipice. He had seen the venturesome Distelfinck jumping along in that direction. He reached there just in time, for at that instant the little goat came to the edge. Just as it was falling, Peter flung himself on the ground and managed to seize one of its legs and hold it fast. Distelfinck bleated with anger and surprise, and struggled obstinately onward.

"Heidi! Help me!" Peter screamed, for he couldn't get up and he was almost pulling off Distelfinck's leg.

Heidi was already there and understood their plight. She pulled some fragrant herbs and held them under Distelfinck's nose.

"Come, Distelfinck," she said soothingly. "You must be sensible. See, you might fall off and break your bones."

The goat quickly turned around and nibbled the herbs from Heidi's hand. Meanwhile Peter had succeeded in getting on his feet and had seized the cord which held the bell around Distelfinck's neck. Heidi seized it on the opposite side, and the two children together led the runaway back to the flock.

When Peter had the goat in safety once more, he raised his rod to beat him soundly as a punishment. Distelfinck timidly drew back, for he saw what was going to happen.

"No, Peter! You must not beat him!" Heidi cried. "See how frightened he is!"

"He deserves it," snarled Peter and was going to strike the goat. But Heidi seized his arm.

"You shall not do it; it will hurt him! Let him alone!"

Peter looked at Heidi in astonishment. Her black eyes were snapping. He reluctantly dropped his rod.

"He can go if you will give me some of your cheese again tomorrow," he said, for he wanted some compensation for his fright.

"You may have it all—the whole piece—tomorrow and every day; I do not want it," said Heidi. "I will give you a good part of my bread, too. But then you must never, never beat Distelfinck, or Schneehöpli, or any of the goats."

"It's all the same to me," said Peter; and this was as good as a promise with him.

By now the sun was ready to go down behind the mountains. Heidi sat on the ground again and gazed at the bluebells and the rock-roses glowing in the evening light. The grass seemed tinted with gold, and the cliffs above began to gleam and sparkle. Suddenly she jumped up and exclaimed:

"Peter! Peter! It's on fire! The mountains are burning, and the big snow field over there and the sky! See! The high cliff is burning! Oh, the beautiful fiery snow! Peter, get up! Everything is on fire!"

"It's always so," said Peter good-naturedly, peeling the bark from his rod, "but it is no fire."

"What is it, then?" asked Heidi, running back and forth. It was so beautiful everywhere she could not see enough.

"It comes so of itself," explained Peter.

"Oh, see! See!" cried Heidi in great excitement. "Suddenly it grows rosy and red! Look at the snow and the high, pointed rocks! What are their names, Peter?"

"Mountains don't have names," he replied.

"How lovely! See the snow all rosy red! And on the rocks above there are ever so many roses! Oh, now they are turning gray! Oh! Oh! Now the rosy light is all gone, Peter." Heidi sat down on the ground, as distressed as if everything was coming to an end.

"It will be just the same again tomorrow," explained Peter. "Get up! We must go home now."

Peter whistled and called the goats together, and they started on the homeward journey.

"Will it be like that every day?" asked Heidi eagerly, as she walked down the mountain by Peter's side.

"Usually," was the reply.

"Tomorrow again?" she wanted to know.

"Yes; yes, tomorrow, certainly!" Peter assured her.

Then Heidi was happy once more, but she had so much to think about that she was silent until they reached the hut and saw her grandfather. He was sitting under the fir trees, where he was in the habit of waiting for his goats. Heidi ran straight up to him, followed by Schwänli and Bärli.

"Come again tomorrow," Peter called.

"I will," Heidi promised, then turned to her grandfather.

"Oh, grandfather, everything was so beautiful—the fire and the roses on the cliffs and the blue and yellow flowers. See what I have brought you!"

Heidi opened her apron, but what a sight met her eyes! The poor little flowers looked like hay, and not a single cup was open.

"What is the matter with them?" she asked, quite shocked.

"They like to stay out in the sunshine and not shut up in your apron," said the grandfather.

"Then I will never bring any more home. But, grandfather, what made the robber-bird scream so?" she asked.

"You must jump into the water now, while I go to the shed and fetch the milk. Afterwards we will go into the house together and have supper. Then I will tell you about it."

Later, when Heidi sat on her high stool before her little bowl of milk, she again asked the question:

"Why did the robber-bird keep croaking and screaming, grandfather?"

"He is mocking at the people down below, because so many sit together in the villages and make one another wicked. So he mocks at them: 'It would be much better for you to leave one another and let each go his own way and climb up to some mountaintop, as I do!'"

The grandfather spoke these words so wildly that Heidi looked at him in surprise.

"Why have the mountains no names, grandfather?" she asked again.

"They have names," he replied. "If you can describe one to me so that I can recognize it, I will tell you what it is called."

Heidi described the rocky mountain, with its two high towers, just as she had seen it, and the grandfather, well pleased, said:

"Very good! I know it; it is called Falkniss (Falcon's nest). Did you see any more?"

So Heidi described the mountain with the big snow field, which had been on fire, then turned rose color, and then suddenly grew pale and wan.

"That is the Cäsaplana," said the grandfather. "So it pleased you up in the pasture, did it?"

"Oh, yes," said Heidi. "But tell me, grandfather, where did the fire at evening come from? Peter did not know."

"The sun does it," the grandfather explained. "When he says good night to the mountains, he sends to them his most beautiful rays so that they may not forget him until he comes back in the morning."

This pleased Heidi. She could hardly wait for another day to come so that she could go up to the pasture and see how the sun said good night to the mountains. But first she had to go to sleep, and she slept soundly the whole night long on her bed of hay, dreaming of mountains and red roses, in the midst of which Schneehöpli merrily ran and jumped.

Chapter 4

AT THE GRANDMOTHER'S

ON THE FOLLOWING morning Peter came with his goats, and Heidi went with him up to the pasture; and so it happened day after day. She grew brown and strong and healthy from this outdoor life, and she was as happy as the birds in the trees.

But when autumn came and the wind blew over the mountains, the grandfather said one morning:

"You must stay here today, Heidi; the wind with one puff could blow a little thing like you down into the valley."

This news made Peter very unhappy. Time passed so slowly when Heidi was not with him, and he missed his hearty dinner. Moreover the goats were so contrary these days and ran off in every direction. They seemed to miss Heidi, too.

As for Heidi, she was never unhappy, for she could always find something about her to enjoy. She would have preferred going with Peter and the goats to the pasture. Still her grandfather's hammering and sawing and carpentering were very interesting. It pleased her that he was just preparing the pretty round goat cheeses. Since she had to stay at home, it was delightful to watch him as he bared both arms and stirred the cheese in the big kettle.

But more attractive than all else to Heidi were the roaring and rushing of the wind in the old fir trees behind the hut. Wherever she happened to be, she had to run to them every little while, for nothing was so fascinating as this deep, mysterious sound in the treetops. She liked to stand under them and listen for an hour at a time.

The sun was no longer hot, as in summer, and Heidi brought out her shoes and stockings and also her little coat.

Then it grew cold, and Peter breathed on his hands when he came early in the morning, but not for long, for suddenly one night a deep snow fell. When the sun rose, the whole Alm was white, and not a single green leaf was to be seen.

After this Peter came no more with his flock. Heidi looked with amazement out of the little window, for it was beginning to snow again. Big flakes fell thick and fast, until the snow came up to the window, and then still higher, until they could not open the window, and they were completely buried in the little house. But by the next day the storm was over, and the grandfather went out with his shovel. He piled up great heaps of snow, so that there seemed to be mountains of it all around the hut.

Now the windows and the door were free. This was fortunate; for as Heidi and her grandfather were sitting in the afternoon on their three-legged stools, suddenly there was a great knocking and stamping against the threshold. The door opened and there stood Peter covered with snow. He had been obliged to struggle through high drifts, so that great lumps remained clinging to him, frozen fast by the cold. But he had not given up, for he was anxious to reach Heidi, whom he had not seen for a whole week.

"Good afternoon," he said, standing as close as possible to the fire. He made no further remark, but his face beamed with pleasure. Heidi looked at him wonderingly, for now that he was so near the fire, he began to thaw out and was dripping like a little waterfall.

"Well, general, how are you?" asked the grandfather. "Now you are without an army and must bite your slate pencil."

"Why must he bite his slate pencil, grandfather?" asked Heidi curiously.

"In winter he has to go to school," explained the grandfather.

"There you learn to read and write, and often it is hard work; so it helps a little if you bite your slate pencil. Isn't it so, general?"

"Yes, it is so," said Peter.

Heidi's interest was aroused, and she had to ask Peter a great many questions about the school. He always found it hard to put his thoughts into words, and this time it was unusually difficult. He had scarcely given one answer before Heidi asked two or more unexpected questions. The corners of the grandfather's mouth were twitching with amusement.

"Well, general," he said, "now you have been under fire and need strengthening. Come, stay to supper with us!"

The grandfather rose and brought the evening meal from the cupboard, and Heidi pushed the stools to the table. Next the wall there was still another seat which the grandfather had made and fastened there. So they all three had good seats; and Peter opened his eyes very wide when he saw what a big piece of the fine dried meat the Alm-Uncle laid on his thick slice of bread. Peter had not had anything so good for a long time.

"Next Sunday I will come again," he told Heidi when he started for home, "and you must come to see my grandmother; she said so."

Heidi had never paid anyone a visit, and she liked the idea. The next morning her first words were:

"Grandfather, I must go down to the grandmother's; she expects me."

"There is too much snow," replied the grandfather, putting her off.

But Heidi did not forget. Not a day passed that she did not say five or six times:

"Grandfather, I really must go; the grandmother is expecting me."

On the fourth day, the cold was so bitter that it crackled with every footstep outdoors. Heidi, as she sat on her high stool eating her dinner, began her little speech again:

"Today I really must go to the grandmother's. She will be tired of waiting for me."

Then the grandfather rose from the dinner table, went up to the hayloft, brought down the thick bag that served as Heidi's bed covering, and said:

"Well, come along!"

The child was delighted and skipped after him out into the glistening world of snow. In the old fir trees, the white snow lay on every bough, and the trees sparkled and shone in the sunshine.

"Oh!" she exclaimed. "The fir trees are covered with silver and gold!"

The grandfather went into the shop but returned a minute later drawing a big sled after him. He wrapped Heidi up in the bag, so she would keep warm, then sat down on the sled and took her in his lap. With his right hand he seized the handle on one side of the sled, and gave a push with both feet. The sled shot away down the mountain so swiftly that Heidi thought she was flying.

Suddenly it stood still in front of Peter's hut. The grandfather put the child on the ground, unwrapped her covering, and said:

"Now go in, and when it begins to grow dark, come out again and start on the way home."

Then he turned round with his sled and drew it up the mountain.

Heidi opened the door and went into a little sitting room. At a table sat a woman mending a jacket, which Heidi recognized as Peter's. In the corner sat an old, bent grandmother spinning. Heidi went up to her at once.

"How do you do, grandmother?" she said. "I have come to see you. Did you think it was a long time before I came?"

The grandmother raised her head and sought for the hand

held out to her.

"Are you the child staying up with the Alm-Uncle?" she asked, "Are you Heidi?"

"Yes, I have just come down with my grandfather on the sled."

"Is that possible? Say, Brigitte, did the Alm-Uncle himself come down with the child?"

Peter's mother, Brigitte, laid down her mending and looked curiously at Heidi.

"I don't know," she said, "whether the uncle himself came with her or not. It does not seem likely. The child may be mistaken."

But Heidi looked straight at the woman and said sturdily:

"I know very well who wrapped me up in the coverlet and brought me down on the sled. It was my grandfather."

"Then there must be something in what Peter told us about the Alm-Uncle," said the grandmother. "Who could have believed that such a thing was possible? I thought the child wouldn't live three weeks up there! How does she look, Brigitte?"

"She has a delicate form like Adelheid," Brigitte replied, "but she has black eyes and curly hair, like Tobias and also like the old man up there."

Meanwhile Heidi had looked around and noticed everything. "See, grandmother," she said. "There is a shutter that keeps swinging back and forth. My grandfather would drive in a nail at once to hold it fast. It will break a pane of glass. See, see!"

"Oh, you good child!" said the grandmother. "I cannot see it, but I can hear it. Everything creaks and rattles when the wind blows. Everything is loose about the hut, but there is no man to mend anything and Peter doesn't know how. Sometimes I can't sleep at night, I am so afraid the house will tumble down on top of our heads."

"But why can't you see how the shutter swings, grandmother? See! There it goes again," and Heidi pointed with her finger.

*The Old, Bent Grandmother Sat in the
Corner Beside Her Spinning Wheel*

"Ah, child! I can see nothing at all, the shutter or anything else," said the grandmother mournfully.

"But if I go out and open the shutter wide so that it will be quite light, can you see then, grandmother?"

"No, not even then! No one can make it light for me again!"

"But if you go out in the white snow, then it will surely be light for you. Just come with me, grandmother; I will show you."

"Let me sit still, you good child! It would be dark to me even in the snow and in the light. My eyes cannot see!"

Heidi burst into loud weeping. "Can no one make it light for you again?" she sobbed. "No one at all?"

"Come, dear Heidi, come here!" said the grandmother, trying to comfort her. "I want to tell you something. When a person cannot see, it is so pleasant to hear a friendly word, and I like to hear you talk. Come, sit down near me and tell me what you do up there and what your grandfather does. I used to know him well."

Heidi quickly wiped away her tears and said comfortingly:

"Just wait, grandmother; I will tell my grandfather all about it. He will make it light for you again, and he will fix the hut so it won't tumble down. He can make everything all right."

The grandmother remained silent. Then Heidi began to tell about her life with her grandfather. She talked about the lovely things he made out of wood—benches and stools and cribs to put hay in for Schwänli and Bärli, and a large new water tub for bathing in summer, and a new milk bowl and spoon. There was nothing Heidi liked better than to stay near the grandfather and watch him at his work.

"Do you hear that, Brigitte?" said the grandmother, "Do you hear what she says of the uncle?"

Suddenly the story was interrupted by a thumping at the door, and in stamped Peter. He opened his eyes wide at the sight of

Heidi, and a good-natured grin spread over his face.

"Is it possible that he has already come home from school!" exclaimed the grandmother. "No afternoon for many a year has passed so quickly! Good afternoon, Peterli! How did you get on with the reading?"

"Just the same," answered Peter.

"Dear, dear!" said the grandmother with a little sigh.

"Why do you look so sad, grandmother?" asked Heidi.

"Up there on the shelf I have an old prayer book," said the grandmother. "It has such beautiful hymns in it, but I have not heard them for so long I cannot remember them. I thought Peterli might learn to read some of the verses to me. But reading seems to be too hard for him; he cannot learn."

"I must get a light," said Peterli's mother. "It is already quite dark. The afternoon has gone before I was aware of it, either."

Heidi jumped up from her chair. "Good night, grandmother! I must go home right away, if it is growing dark."

"Wait, Heidi, Peter will go with you," said the grandmother anxiously. "Take good care of her, Peterli. Don't let her stand still or she might freeze. Has she a good, thick scarf around her neck?"

"I haven't any scarf at all, but I shall not freeze," Heidi called back. Then she went out at the door and slipped away so quickly that Peter could hardly follow her.

The children had gone only a few steps up the mountain when they saw the grandfather coming down, and in a moment he was with them.

"Very good, Heidi," he said. "You have kept your word!" He wrapped the coverlet around the child, took her in his arms and climbed up the mountain. Brigitte saw this and went back into the hut with Peter and told the grandmother all about it.

"God be praised that he is so good to her," said the grandmother. "If he will only let her come again! The child did me so much good."

And until she went to bed she kept repeating: "If she will only come again! Now there is something still left in the world to give me pleasure!"

Meanwhile Heidi, wrapped in her bag, had much to say to her grandfather. "Tomorrow we must take the hammer and the big nails and fasten the shutter at the grandmother's house. Everything creaks and rattles there."

"We must? We must do so? Who told you that?" asked the grandfather.

"Nobody told me," said Heidi, "but everything is loose and the grandmother is afraid when the wind blows. She thinks: 'Now everything will fall down on our heads.' And nobody can make it light any more for the grandmother! Only think how sad it is for her to be always in the dark! Nobody can help her but you! Tomorrow we will go; won't we, grandfather?"

The old man looked at the child thoughtfully. "Yes, Heidi," he said, "we will make everything fast at the grandmother's hut, so that there will be no more rattling. Tomorrow we will do so."

The grandfather kept his word. The following afternoon they took another ride on the sled. The old man set the child down before the door and said, "Now go in, and when it is night come back." Then he laid the bag on the sled and went around the house.

Scarcely had Heidi opened the door and run into the room, when the grandmother called out from her corner:

"Here comes the child! It is the child!"

She stopped the spinning wheel and held out both hands. Heidi pulled up a little low chair quite close.

"Oh, Grandmother," she began, when suddenly she heard a heavy pounding on the house. The grandmother was so frightened she nearly upset the spinning wheel.

"Dear me! it has come at last," she cried. "The hut is tumbling to pieces."

"No, no," said Heidi consolingly. "It is grandfather with his hammer. He is going to mend everything so that you won't be worried and afraid any longer."

"Oh! is it possible? So the dear Lord has not entirely forgotten us!" exclaimed the grandmother. "Did you hear that, Brigitte? Go out and ask the Alm-Uncle to come in so I can thank him."

Brigitte went out just as the Alm-Uncle was driving the fastenings into the wall.

"Good afternoon, uncle," she said. "I want to thank you for doing us such a service, and so does my mother. Surely no one else would do such a thing for us, and—"

"That will do," interrupted the old man. "I know what you think of the Alm-Uncle. Go back into the house. I can find what needs to be done."

Brigitte obeyed, for the uncle had a way which people did not usually oppose. He pounded and hammered all around the hut; then he climbed the narrow little staircase up under the roof and kept on hammering until he had driven the last nail he had brought with him. Meanwhile it had begun to grow dark; he had hardly come down when Heidi came out.

The grandfather wrapped her up in the coverlet and carried her, as on the previous day, drawing the sled after him.

Thus the winter passed. After many long years, happiness had come into the blind grandmother's dreary life. Every day she listened for the tripping footstep, and when the door opened and the child actually came dancing in, then she always exclaimed joyfully:

"God be praised! She has come again!"

Heidi was very fond of the grandmother, but a feeling of sorrow came over the child every time she remembered that no one

—not even the grandfather—could ever make it light for the old lady again. But the grandmother insisted that she was always happy when Heidi was with her, so Heidi came down on the sled every fine winter's day. The grandfather always brought her, and while Heidi was visiting indoors, he spent many an afternoon working on Peter's hut. The result was that there was no more creaking and rattling, and the grandmother declared she would never forget the uncle.

Chapter 5

TWO VISITS AND THEIR CONSEQUENCES

THE WINTER passed quickly, then the summer, and a new winter was drawing to a close. Heidi was eight years old, and twice Peter had brought word from the school teacher in Dörfli that she ought to go to school. But each time the Alm-Uncle had sent back word that he did not intend to send the child to school, and Peter faithfully delivered the message.

One sunny March morning there was a knock on the door, and when Heidi opened it she saw an old man dressed in black.

"You must be Heidi," he said kindly, holding out his hand. "Where is your grandfather?"

"He is sitting at the table, carving round spoons out of wood," replied Heidi, opening the door.

It was the old pastor from Dörfli, who had known the uncle years before. He stepped into the hut, went up to the old man, and said: "Good morning, neighbor!"

The grandfather looked up in surprise. "Good morning, pastor. Won't you sit down?"

"Thank you. I have not seen you for a long time, neighbor."

"Nor have I seen you, pastor," was the answer.

"I came today to talk with you about something," continued the pastor. "I think you already know what it is."

"Heidi, go out to the goats," said the grandfather. "You may take a little salt along and stay with them until I come."

Heidi immediately disappeared.

"The child should have been sent to school a year ago," the

51

pastor went on. "The teacher has sent you word about this several times. What do you intend to do with her, neighbor?"

"I do not intend to send her to school," was the answer.

The pastor gazed with surprise at the old man as he sat with folded arms looking very determined.

"What are you going to make of the child?" the pastor asked.

"Nothing; she grows and thrives with the goats and the birds. She is well enough with them, and she learns no harm with them."

"But the child is neither a goat nor a bird; she is a human being. If she learns no harm from such companions, neither does she learn anything else. I have come to tell you now, neighbor, so you may make your arrangements during the summer. This is the last winter that the child can spend without any instruction. Next winter she must go to school every day."

"I shall not do it, pastor," said the old man decidedly.

"Do you really suppose there are no means of bringing you to terms!" said the pastor somewhat warmly.

"Indeed!" said the old man. "And does the pastor suppose that I would really send a delicate child on icy mornings through storm and snow down the mountain, a two hours' journey, and let her come back again at night? Possibly the pastor can recall her mother, Adelheid; she used to walk in her sleep and have ill turns. Shall the child, too, be made to suffer from such a struggle? Just let anyone come and try to compel me!"

"You are right, neighbor," said the pastor in a more friendly tone. "It would not be possible to send the child from here to school. But I can see that she is dear to you. For her sake do what you ought to have done long ago; come down to Dörfli and live once more with human beings. What kind of a life is this up here, alone and embittered toward God and man?"

The old man shook his head stubbornly. "It is not for me to go down into the valley," he said. "The people down there despise

me and I despise them, so it is better for both that we remain apart."

"No, no; it is not good for you," said the pastor earnestly. "Believe me, neighbor, make peace with God. Ask for his pardon if you have done any wrong. Then come and see how differently the people regard you."

The pastor rose and held out his hand. "I count upon it, neighbor. Next winter you will come down and live among us again, reconciled to God and man."

"The pastor means well," said the Alm-Uncle, "but I cannot do what he expects. I shall not send the child; neither shall I come down myself."

"Then God help you!" said the pastor, and went sadly out of the hut and down the mountain.

The Alm-Uncle was out of sorts. In the afternoon when Heidi said, "Now let us go to the grandmother's," he replied curtly, "Not today."

He did not speak again all day, and the following morning

when Heidi asked, "Are we going to the grandmother's?" he merely said, "We shall see."

Before the bowls had been put away after dinner another visitor came to the door. It was Aunt Dete wearing a fine hat with a feather. The uncle looked her over from head to toe but said not a word.

Aunt Dete began to talk, just as though she was saying a speech she had rehearsed. She tried to flatter the uncle by saying Heidi looked so well that she hardly recognized her. It was plain to be seen that the child had fared well with her grandfather. But she must be a great deal of trouble to him, and Dete had come to take her away.

"I have such good news for Heidi I can hardly believe it myself," she said. "Some wealthy relatives of my mistress, who live in almost the finest house in Frankfurt, have an only daughter who is obliged to sit all the time in a wheel chair, because she is lame. She has to study alone with a teacher, and this is very dull for her. Besides she would like to have a playmate in the house, and the housekeeper told my mistress that they were looking for a nice, unspoiled child. Of course, I thought of Heidi at once, and I hurried over and told the lady all about the child and her character. The lady engaged to have her come, and it is a wonderful piece of good luck for Heidi. If she pleases the people and anything should happen to the only daughter—you know she is so sickly—who knows but that—"

"Will you ever finish?" interrupted the uncle, who had not said a word all this time.

"Bah," retorted Dete, tossing her head. "You act exactly as if I had told you the most ordinary thing in the world. There isn't a single person in all Prättigau who wouldn't thank God if I brought such news to them as I have brought to you."

"Take it to anyone you like; I will have none of it," said the uncle bluntly.

Dete went off like a rocket.

"Well, if that is what you think about it, uncle," she said, "I will tell you what I think. The child is eight years old and you will not send her to school or to church; that they told me down in Dörfli. She is my own sister's child. I have to answer for what happens to her; and when a child can have such a good fortune as Heidi, I won't give in. There isn't a person down in Dörfli who will not help me. So take heed if you don't care to be brought before the court, uncle. There are things that might be brought up which you would not like to hear, for when a man once gets into court many things are hunted up that he has forgotten all about."

"Silence!" roared the uncle, and his eyes blazed. "Take her and be gone! Never bring her into my sight again. I never want to see her with feathers in her hat and words in her mouth such as you have spoken today!"

The uncle strode out of the house.

"You have made my grandfather angry," said Heidi, and her black eyes snapped.

"He will soon be all right again. Now come," urged the aunt. "Where are your clothes?"

"I will not come," said Heidi.

"Come along. You can't imagine what a good time you will have." Aunt Dete went to the cupboard and took out Heidi's things. "Come, put on your hat for we shall have to hurry."

"I shall not come," answered Heidi again.

"Don't be so foolish and stubborn, like the goats; you must have learned it from them. Listen to me. Your grandfather is angry; you have just heard him say that we must never come into his sight again. He wants you to go with me now, and you must not make him more angry. You haven't the least idea how lovely it is in Frankfurt or how many things you will see there. If you don't like it you can come back here; then the grandfather will be good-natured again."

"Can I come back again tonight?"

"Oh, come along! I tell you, you can come home if you want to. Today we will go as far as Mayenfeld, and tomorrow morning early we will get into the train. In that you can get home again in no time; it's like flying."

Aunt Dete took the bundle of clothes on her arm, and Heidi by the hand, and they started down the mountain. Just as they passed the goatherd's hut, they met Peter coming home from school.

"Where are you going?" he asked.

"I am hurrying to Frankfurt with my aunt," replied Heidi, "but first I will go in to see the grandmother for she is expecting me today."

"No, no talking; it is too late," said the aunt hastily, holding the struggling Heidi fast by the hand. "You can see her when you come back; so come along!"

Whereupon the aunt dragged Heidi off and would not let go her hand. She was afraid if the child went into the hut she might refuse to leave and the grandmother would take her part. Peter ran indoors and beat on the table with his fists, making such a frightful noise that the little house trembled. The grandmother sprang up from her spinning wheel in alarm and cried out.

"What is the matter, Peterli? What makes you act so wild?" asked his mother patiently.

"She has taken Heidi away with her," explained Peter.

"Where, Peterli, where?" cried the grandmother, groping her way toward the window. She guessed what had happened, for Brigitte had seen Dete go up to the Alm-Uncle's. Trembling in her haste, the grandmother opened the window and called out be-

seechingly:

"Dete, Dete, don't take the child away from us! Don't take Heidi away from us!"

The two travelers heard the voice, but Dete took hold of the child more firmly than ever and ran as fast as she could.

"The grandmother is calling; I want to go to her," said Heidi, drawing back.

But the aunt pacified her by saying they must hurry on to Frankfurt. If Heidi wanted to she could bring the grandmother a present. This prospect pleased Heidi. She began to hurry without further objection.

"What can I bring home to the grandmother?" she asked after a while.

"Something good," said the aunt. "Some lovely, soft white rolls will please her, for she can hardly eat the hard black bread any longer."

"Yes; she always gives it back to Peter because it is too hard for her," said Heidi. "So let us go fast, Aunt Dete. Then, perhaps, we shall reach Frankfurt today, and I can soon be back with the rolls."

Heidi began to run so fast that Dete could hardly keep up with her. But she was very glad that she went so swiftly, for they were coming to the first houses in Dörfli. Heidi pulled so hard at her hand that everyone could see that she had to hurry to please the child. So when people tried to stop her and ask her questions, she merely said:

"I can't stop now, for the child is in a hurry, and we have far to go."

"Are you taking her away? Is she running away from the Alm-Uncle? It's a wonder that she is still alive! And yet what rosy cheeks she has!"

Such remarks as these came from every side; and Dete was glad not to have to stop and make any explanations. Heidi did not seem to hear but only pushed on in greater haste.

From that day on the Alm-Uncle looked more ill-natured than ever when he came down to Dörfli, with his cheese basket on his back. He spoke to no one as he passed through the village on his way down to the valley to sell his cheeses and lay in his supply of bread and meat. He looked so wild with his thick brows and his enormous staff that people said his grandchild had been very fortunate to escape. They had seen how she hurried away as if she were afraid the old man was coming after her to bring her back.

The blind grandmother was the only one who stood by the Alm-Uncle. She always told everyone who came up to her house, to bring spinning or to get yarn, how good he had been to the child, and what he had done for her and her daughter. So this information also reached Dörfli; but most people said that perhaps the grandmother was too old to understand, for she could no longer hear well, and she could not see at all.

The Alm-Uncle showed himself no more at Peter's hut. It was a good thing that it had been so well repaired, for it remained for a long time untouched.

And not a day passed that the grandmother did not say, "Ah, the days are so empty without the child. If I could only hear Heidi's voice once more before I die!"

Chapter 6

NEW SCENES

~~~~~~

IN THE HOUSE of Herr Sesemann, in Frankfurt, reclined the little sick daughter, Klara, in her comfortable wheel chair. She spent the whole day in it and was pushed from one room to another. She had a pale, thin face and gentle blue eyes.

"Isn't it time for them to come yet, Fräulein Rottenmeier?" she asked anxiously, looking at the clock on the library wall.

Fräulein Rottenmeier sat upright in a little sewing chair embroidering. She wore a mysterious wrap, a large cape, which gave her a solemn appearance, and was accentuated by a kind of high dome, which she had on her head. Klara's mother was dead and Herr Sesemann was away most of the time, and Fräulein Rottenmeier was in charge of the household.

"Isn't it time *yet*?" said the usually patient Klara again.

At that moment Tinette, a scornful-looking maid wearing a little white cap, appeared in the doorway. She was followed a moment later by Dete, holding Heidi by the hand.

Fräulein Rottenmeier slowly rose from her seat and came nearer. The child's appearance did not seem to please her. Heidi had on her plain cotton dress and her old crushed straw hat. She looked up with unconcealed amazement at the dome-like cap on the lady's head.

"What is your name?" asked Fräulein Rottenmeier.

"Heidi," was the reply.

"What? That can surely be no Christian name. What name was given you in baptism?" asked Fräulein Rottenmeier.

"That I do not know," said Heidi.

"What an answer!" exclaimed the lady, shaking her head. "Dete, is the child foolish or pert?"

"If the lady will allow me, I will speak for the child," said Dete, giving Heidi a little nudge on the sly for her unbecoming answer. "She is neither foolish nor pert, but this is the first time she has ever been in a gentleman's house, and she knows nothing about good manners. She is willing and quick to learn if the lady will have forbearance. She was baptized Adelheid, like her mother, my late sister."

"Well! That is a name that can be pronounced," said Fräulein Rottenmeier. "But, Dete, I told you that Fräulein Klara's companion must be of her age, in order to pursue the same studies. Fräulein Klara is more than twelve years old. This child looks several years younger."

"With the lady's permission," Dete began again, "I can't recollect just how old she is. To be sure, she must be somewhat younger, but not much. I can't say exactly; but she may be about ten or nearly that, I should think."

"I am eight now; grandfather said so," explained Heidi. The aunt nudged her again; but Heidi was not at all embarrassed.

"What? Only eight years old!" exclaimed Fräulein Rottenmeier with some indignation. "Four years too young! What have you learned? And what books have you studied?"

"None," said Heidi.

"What? How did you learn to read then?" asked the lady again.

"I have never learned to read; neither has Peter," stated Heidi.

"Good gracious! You cannot read! You really cannot read!" exclaimed Fräulein Rottenmeier in horror. "What have you learned, then?"

"Nothing," said Heidi truthfully.

"Dete," said Fräulein Rottenmeier, "this is not according to the agreement. How could you bring me this creature?"

But Dete was not easily abashed; she answered eagerly; "The child is exactly what I thought the lady wanted. The lady explained to me that she must be quite different and not at all like other children; so I brought this little one. But I must be going. My mistress is expecting me."

With a courtesy Dete went out of the door and down the stairs as fast as she could go. Fräulein Rottenmeier stood still for a moment, then ran after Dete. Heidi remained standing by the door until Klara, who had been watching her in silence, beckoned. Then she went over and stood by the wheel chair.

"Would you rather be called Heidi or Adelheid?" asked Klara.

"My name is Heidi and nothing else," was the reply.

"Then I will always call you that," said Klara. "I like the name. I never heard it before, but I have never seen a child before that looks like you. Have you always had such short, curly hair?"

"Yes, I think so," answered Heidi.

"Did you want to come to Frankfurt?" asked Klara.

"No. Tomorrow I am going home to carry the grandmother some white rolls," explained Heidi.

"You are a strange child!" said Klara. "They have brought you to Frankfurt expressly to stay with me and study with me. It will be very funny, because you don't know how to read at all, and there will be something entirely new in the study hours. You see, the Herr Kandidat comes every morning at ten o'clock, and then the lessons last until two, and the time seems so long. But now it will be less tiresome, because I can listen while you learn to read."

Heidi shook her head when she heard about learning to read.

"But Heidi, you must learn to read, of course, everyone has to," said Klara.

Just then Fräulein Rottenmeier came back, evidently much disturbed because she had not been able to overtake Dete and call

her back. Sebastian, the butler, with big round eyes like Peter's, opened the double doors leading from the dining room and pushed Klara's wheel chair out to the table. Heidi placed herself in front of him and looked up in astonishment.

"You look just like Peter, the goatherd," she said.

Fräulein Rottenmeier clasped her hands in horror. "Is it possible?" she groaned. "She is talking to the servants! The creature lacks even the most primitive ideas!"

Sebastian rolled Klara's chair up to the table. Fräulein Rottenmeier sat next her and beckoned to Heidi to take the place opposite. By Heidi's plate lay a lovely white roll; the child cast longing looks at it. When Sebastian held out the large tray and offered her the fried fish, she pointed to the roll.

"Can I have that?" she asked.

Sebastian nodded, and Heidi seized her roll and put it in her pocket. Sebastian made a face to keep from laughing, for he knew very well that it was not allowable. He remained standing silently by Heidi, waiting for her to serve herself. She looked up at him in amazement.

"Shall I eat some of that?"

Sebastian nodded again.

"Then give me some," she said, looking calmly at her plate.

Sebastian's face grew very thoughtful, and the tray in his hand began to tremble dangerously.

"You can put the tray on the table and come back later," said Fräulein Rottenmeier, looking at him severely.

Sebastian at once disappeared.

"As for you, Adelheid, I see I must tell you how to behave at table," said Fräulein Rottenmeier with a sigh, and she explained clearly and minutely everything Heidi had to do.

"I must impress on you," she finished, "that you are not to speak to Sebastian at the table, unless you have some order to give, or some necessary question to ask."

She then told her how she was to address the different members of the household, ending with: "Klara will tell you what she wishes you to call her."

"Klara, of course," said the little invalid.

Then followed a multitude of instructions about rising in the morning and going to bed, about coming in and going out, about shutting doors, and about orderliness in general. Meantime Heidi's eyes closed, for she had been up since five o'clock and had taken a long journey. She leaned back in her chair and fell asleep. When Fräulein Rottenmeier finally came to the end of her instructions, she said:

"Now think this all over! Have you understood everything?"

"Heidi has been asleep for a long time," said Klara, looking much amused; the supper hour had not passed so quickly in a long time.

"I never in all my life saw the like of this child!" exclaimed Fräulein Rottenmeier in great vexation; and she rang the bell so violently that Tinette and Sebastian both came rushing in together. In spite of all the confusion Heidi did not wake, and they had the greatest difficulty in arousing her sufficiently to get her to bed.

Chapter 7

FRÄULEIN ROTTENMEIER HAS AN UNCOMFORTABLE DAY

HEIDI was lying in a high white bed in a large room. Near by stood two chairs and a sofa with large flowers on them. In the corner was a washstand, and there were things on it which Heidi had never seen before.

Suddenly she remembered that she was in Frankfurt, and she jumped out of bed and dressed. She went first to one window and then to the other, for she wanted to see the sky and earth outside; she felt as if she were in a cage behind the long curtains. She could not push them aside, so she crawled in behind them in order to reach the window. But this was too high for her to see out. Like a little bird placed for the first time in a handsome cage, she flew from one window to another. She wanted to see something besides walls. She felt that she must see the green grass and the last melting snows on the cliffs.

There was a knock on the door, and Tinette thrust in her head. "Breakfast's ready!" she said curtly.

Heidi did not understand that these words meant an invitation. Tinette's scornful face seemed to warn her not to come too near, and Heidi acted accordingly. She took the little footstool out from under the table, placed it in a corner, sat down on it, and waited to see what would happen. After some time she heard a bustling, and Fräulein Rottenmeier came into the room.

"What is the matter with you, Adelheid? Don't you understand what breakfast means? Come down!"

Heidi understood this, and followed her at once.

Klara was waiting in the dining room and gave Heidi a friendly greeting. She looked much more contented than usual, for she expected all sorts of strange things to happen that day. The breakfast passed without any disturbance. Heidi ate her bread and butter properly enough, and after the meal was over Klara was rolled back into the library. When the two children were alone Heidi said at once:

"How do you see outdoors and 'way down to the ground here?"

"We open the windows and look out," replied Klara, amused at the question.

"I can't reach them," said Heidi.

"Ask Sebastian. He will open them for you," said Klara.

Then Klara asked Heidi about her home; and Heidi felt almost happy again when she began to talk about the Alm.

In the meantime the Herr Kandidat had arrived and Fräulein Rottenmeier took him into the dining room. She told him how Herr Sesemann had asked her to find a companion for his daughter, and how disappointed she was in the child who had come. It would be necessary for the Herr Kandidat to begin his instructions with the alphabet. She suggested that he tell Herr Sesemann that the two children could not be taught together without great harm to the more advanced pupil. Then she was sure that the master of the house would be willing to have the strange child sent away.

But the Herr Kandidat was very discreet. He tried to say a few consoling words to Fräulein Rottenmeier but said he would be glad to undertake to teach the new child her ABC's. Then he opened the door and went into the library.

Fräulein Rottenmeier strode up and down the room, considering how the servants should address Adelheid. But she was not to meditate long, for suddenly from the library came a frightful crash. She rushed into the room. There on the floor everything lay in a heap—books, copy books, inkstand, and on top of all the rest the tablecover.

Heidi had disappeared.

"Just look at that!" exclaimed Fräulein Rottenmeier, wringing her hands. "Table cover, books, and work-basket, all covered with ink. It must be that wretched child again."

The Herr Kandidat stood looking at the destruction in dismay, but Klara seemed delighted.

"Yes, Heidi did it," she said, "but not on purpose, so she must not be blamed. She was in such a hurry to get away, she pulled the cover with her, and everything fell with it to the floor. Several carriages went by, and she rushed out. Perhaps she had never seen a coach before."

"There, isn't it just as I told you, Herr Kandidat? The creature hasn't an idea about anything! Not a suspicion what a lesson hour is, and that she ought to sit still and listen. But where is the child? If she has run away, what would Herr Sesemann say to me?"

Fräulein Rottenmeier darted out and down the stairs. There in the open doorway stood Heidi, looking, quite perplexed, up and down the street.

"What is the matter with you? Why have you run away?" demanded Fräulein Rottenmeier.

"I heard the fir trees roar, but I don't know where they are, and I don't hear them any longer," answered Heidi sadly. The noise of the rolling carriages had died away. Heidi had mistaken this sound for the wind blowing through the fir trees, and she had wanted to see them.

"Firs! Are we in the woods? What a notion! Come up and see what you have done!"

Heidi followed Fräulein Rottenmeier upstairs and was very much astonished to see the great damage done. In her haste to hear the fir trees she had not noticed what she was dragging.

"When you are having lessons, you must sit still in your chair and pay attention," said Fräulein Rottenmeier. "If you cannot do it by yourself, I shall have to fasten you to your seat. Do you understand?"

"Yes, I will sit still now," replied Heidi, for she began to comprehend what she was expected to do.

In the afternoon Klara always had to take a long nap, and Heidi was told that she could do as she pleased. She already had a plan, so she waited in the hall until she had a chance to speak with Sebastian.

"I would like to ask you something," she said.

"All right, go ahead, Mamsell," he answered.

"My name isn't Mamsell. My name is Heidi."

"That's all right. Fräulein Rottenmeier told me to call you so," explained Sebastian.

"Did she? Well, then, I must be called so," said Heidi resignedly, for she had noticed that everything had to be as Fräulein Rottenmeier wished.

"Now I have three names," she added with a sigh.

"What did the little Mamsell want to ask?" said Sebastian.

"How do you open the windows, Sebastian?"

"This way," he replied, leading the way to the dining room and swinging out one of the big windows. Heidi went to it, but her head barely reached the sill.

"There; now the little girl can look out and see what there is below," said Sebastian, bringing a high wooden stool and setting it down. Heidi climbed up with great delight, and was able at last to take the longed-for look out the window.

"But there is nothing to see," she said in a disappointed voice, "except the stony street. What is there on the other side of the house, Sebastian?"

"Just the same," was the answer.

"But where do you go to see way down across the whole valley?"

"You have to climb up into some high church tower, like the one over there with the golden dome. From up there you can see away off ever so far."

Then Heidi climbed down from the stool, ran out of the door, down the stairs, and went out into the street. But she did not find it as she imagined it would be. When she saw the tower through the window, she fancied she would only have to go across the street and it would be just in front of her. She went down the entire length of the street, without coming to the tower. She could no longer see it anywhere. She came to another street and then another, but still she did not see the tower. A great many persons passed her, but they were all in such a hurry that Heidi thought they would have no time to talk to her. Finally she saw a boy standing on the corner of the next street. He was carrying a small hand organ on his back and a strange animal in his arms, Heidi ran up to him and asked:

"Where is the tower with the golden dome? Won't you show

me where it is?"

"Show me first what you will give me if I do."

The boy held out his hand. Heidi searched in her pocket. She drew out a little picture, on which was painted a garland of red roses. She disliked to part with it, for Klara had given it to her that morning. But more than anything she wanted to look down into the valley across the green slopes.

"Will you take that?" asked Heidi, holding out the picture. The boy shook his head.

"What do you want, then?" asked Heidi, delighted to put her picture back into her pocket.

"Money."

"I haven't any, but Klara has, and she will give me some. How much do you want?"

"Twenty pfennigs."

"Well, then, come along."

The two went through a long street, and Heidi asked her companion what he was carrying on his back. He explained that under the cloth he had an organ which made wonderful music when he turned the handle. At last they came to an old church with a high tower.

"There!" said the boy.

Heidi noticed a bell in the wall and pulled it with all her might. "You must wait for me, because I don't know the way back," she said.

"What will you give me if I do?"

"What shall I have to give you?"

"Twenty pfennigs more."

A key was turned in the lock on the inside, and the creaking door opened. An old man stepped out and looked at first surprised and then angry.

"How did you dare to ring for me to come down?" he said,

"Can't you read what it says under the bell? 'For those who wish to ascend the tower.'"

Heidi replied, "I want to go up into the tower."

"What do you want to do up there?" asked the towerkeeper.

"I want to go up so that I can look down," she answered.

"Go home, and don't play any more tricks on me, or you won't get off so easily another time!" Whereupon the towerkeeper turned round and was about to shut the door, but Heidi held him by the coattail.

"Only just this once!" she begged.

She looked up at him so beseechingly he changed his mind. Taking the child's hand he said kindly:

"If you are so anxious to go, come with me."

The boy sat down on the stone step in front of the door to wait. Heidi, holding the towerkeeper's hand, climbed many, many steps, which grew smaller and smaller. Finally she went up an extremely narrow staircase, and then she was at the top. The keeper lifted her up to the open window.

"There, now look down," he said.

Heidi saw below her a sea of roofs, towers, and chimneys.

"It is not at all what I thought it would be," she said in a tone of disappointment.

"Is that so? What does a little girl like you know about a view? Well, now come down, and don't ring at a church door again!"

The keeper put Heidi on the floor and started down the narrow stairs in front of her. On the left, where they began to grow wider, there was a door which opened into the keeper's room. Close by, where the floor extended out under the sloping roof, stood a large basket, and in front of it sat a big gray cat.

"You may look at the kittens, if you like," said the towerkeeper. "They're in the basket."

Heidi went toward the basket and screamed with delight.

"Oh, the cunning little creatures!" she exclaimed again and again, running back and forth around the basket, to watch the eight little kittens as they crawled and jumped and tumbled over one another.

"Would you like one?" asked the towerkeeper.

"For my own? To keep always?" asked Heidi, hardly able to believe in such good luck.

"Yes, to be sure. You can have them all, if you have room for them," said the man, glad of a chance to dispose of the kittens.

Heidi was delighted. The kittens would have so much room in the big house, and how surprised and pleased Klara would be.

"But how can I carry them?" asked Heidi.

"I will bring them to you; only tell me where," said the keeper.

"To Herr Sesemann's big house. There is a golden head of a dog with a big ring in his mouth on the front door," explained Heidi.

"I know where it is, but whom shall I ask for? You don't belong to Herr Sesemann, do you?"

"No; but Klara will be delighted to have them. If I could only carry one or two with me—one for myself and one for Klara! Why can't I?"

"Help yourself," said the keeper, and Heidi's eyes shone with delight. She chose a white kitten and a striped yellow and white one, and put one in her right pocket and the other in the left. Then she went down the stairs.

The boy was still sitting on the steps outside. He started off on a run, with Heidi after him, and in a short time they stood directly in front of Herr Sesemann's house. Heidi rang the bell. Sebastian soon appeared, and when he saw Heidi he exclaimed urgently:

"Quick! Quick!"

Heidi ran in in great haste, and Sebastian closed the door. He had not noticed the boy standing disappointed, outside.

"Quick, Mamsell!" said Sebastian. "Go right into the dining room. They are already at the table. Fräulein Rottenmeier looks like a loaded cannon; but what made the little Mamsell run away so?"

Heidi went into the dining room. Fräulein Rottenmeier did not look up, and Klara said nothing. There was an uncomfortable silence. Sebastian pushed up Heidi's chair.

"Adelheid, I will talk with you later," said Fräulein Rottenmeier sternly. "Now I have only this to say: you have behaved very badly, and deserve to be punished for leaving the house without asking permission. I never heard of such conduct."

"Meow," sounded as the apparent answer.

Then the lady grew angry.

"What, Adelheid," she exclaimed, raising her voice, "after such behavior, do you dare to play a naughty trick? You had better be careful, I assure you!"

"I didn't," began Heidi.

"Meow! Meow!"

Sebastian put his tray down on the table and rushed out of the room.

"Leave the table," said Fräulein Rottenmeier furiously.

Heidi, much frightened, rose from her chair and tried once more to explain.

"I really didn't—"

"Meow! Meow! Meow!"

"But Heidi," said Klara, "when you see how angry you are making Fräulein Rottenmeier, why do you keep saying, 'Meow'?"

"I am not doing it; it is the kittens," Heidi was able to speak at last without interruption.

"What? Cats? Kittens?" screamed Fräulein Rottenmeier. "Sebastian! Tinette! Find the horrible creatures and take them away!"

Whereupon the lady rushed into the library and fastened the door in order to be safe, for to Fräulein Rottenmeier kittens were the most dreadful things in the world. Sebastian was standing outside the door and had to stop laughing before he could enter the room again. While he was serving Heidi, he had noticed a little cat's head peeping out of her pocket, and when it began to meow he could hardly contain himself long enough to set his tray on the table.

At last he was able to go back calmly into the room. By this time everything was quiet and peaceful; Klara was holding the kittens in her lap, and Heidi was kneeling by her side, playing with the two tiny, graceful creatures.

"Sebastian," said Klara, "you must help us. You must find a bed for the kittens where Fräulein Rottenmeier will not see them, for she is afraid of them, and will have them taken away."

"I will take care of them, Fräulein Klara," replied Sebastian willingly. "I will make a fine bed for them in a basket, and put it where the timid lady will never come. Just leave it all to me."

Sebastian went on with his work, chuckling to himself, for he did not at all dislike to see Fräulein Rottenmeier a little distressed.

"Have the horrible creatures been taken away?" called Fräulein Rottenmeier through a crack in the door.

"Yes, indeed!" answered Sebastian. Quickly he took the two kittens out of Klara's lap and disappeared with them.

Chapter 8

DISTURBANCES IN THE SESEMANN HOUSE

On the following morning Sebastian had no sooner opened the front door for the Herr Kandidat and ushered him into the library than someone else rang the bell. When he opened the door, he saw a ragged boy with a hand organ on his back.

"What do you mean?" said Sebastian. "I will teach you how to pull doorbells! What do you want here?"

"I want to see Klara," was the reply.

"You dirty urchin, you! Can't you say 'Fräulein Klara,' as the rest of us do? What have you to do with Fräulein Klara?"

"She owes me forty centimes," explained the boy. "I showed her the way yesterday; that makes twenty centimes. Then I showed her the way back that makes twenty more!"

"You see what a fib you are telling. Fräulein Klara never goes out; she is not able to go out."

"But I saw her on the street," said the boy. "She had short, curly black hair, and her eyes are black, and her dress brown, and she doesn't talk as we do."

"Oho!" thought Sebastian, chuckling to himself. "That is the little Mamsell, who has been in more mischief.

"All right," he said aloud. "Wait here at the door until I come back. If I let you come in, you must play something. It will please Fräulein Klara."

He went upstairs and knocked at the library door.

"There is a boy here who wishes to see Fräulein Klara herself," he announced.

Klara was very much delighted at this unusual occurrence. "He may come in," she said. "May he not, Herr Kandidat, if he wants to speak to me?"

The boy soon entered the room, and, according to his instructions, began to play his organ. Fräulein Rottenmeier, busy in the dining room, stopped to listen, hardly able to believe her ears. When she threw open the library door, she could hardly believe her eyes either. In the middle of the floor stood a ragged organ-grinder, playing his instrument. The Herr Kandidat seemed trying to say something, but the words failed to come. Klara and Heidi were listening with beaming faces to the music.

"Stop! Stop immediately!" exclaimed Fräulein Rottenmeier, but her voice was drowned by the music. She ran toward the boy, but suddenly felt something between her feet. She looked on the floor; a horrible black creature was crawling under her skirts —a turtle. Fräulein Rottenmeier jumped in the air as she had not done for many years, and screamed at the top of her voice:

"Sebastian! Sebastian!"

The organ-grinder stopped, for this time her voice was heard above the music. Sebastian, doubled up with laughter, stood outside the half-open door, for he had seen Fräulein Rottenmeier jump. Finally he entered. Fräulein Rottenmeier had thrown herself into a chair.

"Away with them both, the boy and that creature! Send them away immediately, Sebastian!" she cried.

The boy seized his turtle and followed Sebastian down the stairs. At the door Sebastian pressed something into his hand.

"Forty for Fräulein Klara," he said, "and forty for playing. You did well."

Studies were resumed in the library, and Fräulein Rottenmeier settled down to watch. When lessons were over, she was determined to find out who had brought the organ-grinder boy into

the house.

Soon there came another knock at the door, and Sebastian carried in a large, covered basket. Someone has brought it to Fräulein Klara, he said.

"To me?" asked Klara in surprise. "Let me see at once what it looks like."

"I think you had better finish your studies first and then open the basket," remarked Fräulein Rottenmeier.

Klara could not imagine what had been sent to her; and she gazed with longing eyes at the basket.

"Herr Kandidat," she said, stopping short while she was declining a word, "may I not take just one little peep to see what is in the basket and then go right on with my lessons?"

"From one point of view I might be in favor of it, from another against it," replied the Herr Kandidat. "The reason for it would be that if your whole attention is directed toward this object—"

His remark was never finished. The cover of the basket was not fastened, and suddenly, one, two, three, and then two more little kittens jumped out into the room and began to scamper around. They jumped over the Herr Kandidat's boots, bit his trousers, climbed up Fräulein Rottenmeier's dress, crawled around her feet, leaped up into Klara's chair, scratched, groped about, and mewed. Klara was enraptured.

"Oh, what cunning little creatures!" she exclaimed. "Look, Heidi, here, there! Look at that one!"

Heidi ran after the kittens into every corner. The Herr Kandidat stood by the table, lifting first one foot and then the other. Fräulein Rottenmeier at first sat speechless with horror; then she began to scream at the top of her voice:

"Tinette! Tinette! Sebastian! Sebastian!"

Finally Sebastian and Tinette answered her repeated calls for help. They put the kittens, one after another, back into the basket and carried them to the bed made for the two kittens that had arrived the night before.

That evening when Fräulein Rottenmeier had recovered sufficiently from the excitement of the morning, she called Sebastian and Tinette into the library. Then it came out that indirectly Heidi had been the cause of all that had happened. After the servants had left the room, Fräulein Rottenmeier turned to the child, who stood by Klara's chair unaware that she had done anything wrong.

"Adelheid," she said severely, "I know only one punishment which could have any effect on you. We shall see whether you become civilized in the dark cellar with lizards and rats, so that you will never let such things happen again."

Heidi listened calmly to her sentence. The room adjoining the Alm hut, which her grandfather called the cellar, and where the cheese and fresh milk were kept, was a pleasant, inviting place, and she had never seen any rats and lizards.

But Klara raised great objection. "No, no, Fräulein Rottenmeier," she cried, "you must wait until papa is here. He is coming soon, and I shall tell him everything. Then he will say what is to be done with Heidi."

Fräulein Rottenmeier rose, saying somewhat bitterly:

"Very well, Klara, but I, too, shall have a word to say to Herr Sesemann."

Whereupon she left the room.

Several peaceful days followed, but Fräulein Rottenmeier did not get over her distress. It seemed to her that everything had gone wrong since Heidi came.

Klara was contented. The days no longer seemed dull, and Heidi made the study hours pass quickly. The alphabet always confused her and she could never learn it. When the Herr Kandidat was in the midst of explaining and writing the forms of the letters, and in order to make them clearer, compared one to a little horn and another to a beak, she would exclaim with delight, "It is a goat!" or "It is the robber-bird!" The description awakened all sorts of memories, but no idea of the alphabet.

In the late afternoon hours Heidi would sit beside Klara and tell all about the Alm. Then her longing for it became so intense that she would cry out:

"I really must go home now! Tomorrow I must go!"

But Klara always told Heidi that she must remain until the papa came home; then they would see what would happen.

Heidi was very happy about one thing. Every noon and night a lovely white roll lay by her place, and she immediately put this in her pocket. She was saving these rolls to take to the blind grandmother.

Every day after dinner Heidi sat for two long hours alone in her room, for she was not allowed to run outdoors in Frankfurt as she did on the Alm. Neither did she dare to talk to Sebastian in the dining room, for Fräulein Rottenmeier had forbidden that also. So Heidi sat thinking to herself how the Alm was growing green again, how the yellow flowers were glistening in the sunshine, and how bright everything was—the snow and the mountains and the whole wide valley. She often felt as if she could not bear it any longer, so great was her yearning to be there. Her aunt had told her, moreover, that she might go home whenever she liked.

So it happened that one day she packed up her rolls in great haste in the big red neckerchief, put on her straw hat and started. At the very door she encountered Fräulein Rottenmeier just returning from a walk.

"What does this mean?" she cried. "Have I not forbidden you to go wandering about again? Now you are trying to start out another time, looking for all the world like a tramp."

"I am not going to wander about. I only want to go home," replied Heidi, frightened.

"What? You want to go home?" Fräulein Rottenmeier wrung her hands in her agitation. "Run away! If Herr Sesemann knew that! Are you not better treated than you deserve? Is there anything you need? Have you ever in your whole life had a home, or a table or the service that you have here? Tell me!"

"No," replied Heidi.

"I know that perfectly well," continued the lady in great excitement. "You are the most ungrateful child I ever heard of."

Then all Heidi's pent-up feelings broke forth.

"Indeed I am going home, for I have been away so long that Schneehöpli must be crying for me all the time, and the grandmother is expecting me, and Distelfinck will be beaten if Peter has no cheese, and here you never see how the sun says good night to the mountains. If the robber-bird should fly over Frankfurt he would scream still louder, because so many people live together and make each other wicked, and do not go up on the cliffs where it would be good for them."

"Mercy, the child is crazy!" exclaimed Fräulein Rottenmeier. She darted in alarm up the stairs and ran hard against Sebastian, who was coming down.

"Bring up that miserable creature at once!" she said, pointing to Heidi.

Heidi still stood, with flaming eyes, on the same spot, and her whole body trembled with excitement.

"Pshaw! The little Mamsell must not take it so to heart," said Sebastian, patting her on the shoulder. "We must go upstairs now; she said so."

Heidi went up the stairs, very slowly and quietly, and not at all as she was wont to go. That made Sebastian feel sorry. He went behind her and spoke encouraging words to her.

"You mustn't be so sad!" he said. "Only be brave about it! We have had a very sensible little Mamsell, who has never cried since she has been with us. By and by we'll go to see the kittens when the lady in there is away. Then you'll feel better."

Heidi nodded her head slightly, but so sadly that it went to Sebastian's heart. He looked at her compassionately as she stole away to her room.

Fräulein Rottenmeier felt calmer the next day. Late in the afternoon she remembered how shabby Heidi had looked when she had tried to go home. She was determined to replenish the child's wardrobe, before Herr Sesemann came back, with some of Klara's clothes. She talked to Klara about it, and the little girl gladly picked out a number of hats and dresses that she wanted Heidi to have. But first Fräulein Rottenmeier decided to look in Heidi's closet and see what the child already had. Then she could determine what clothes should be kept and what disposed of. In a few moments she came back again, looking very much disgusted.

"What a discovery I have made, Adelheid!" she exclaimed. "In your closet, a clothes closet, Adelheid, in the bottom of this closet, what do I find? A pile of little rolls! Bread, I say, Klara, in a clothes closet! And such a pile stowed away!

"Tinette!" she called into the dining room, "take away the old bread in Adelheid's closet and the crushed straw hat on the table."

"No! No!" screamed Heidi. "I must have the hat, and the rolls are for the grandmother." She was about to rush after Tinette, but was held fast by Fräulein Rottenmeier.

"Stay here and the rubbish will be put where it belongs," she said decidedly. Heidi threw herself down by Klara's chair, sobbing in despair:

"Now the grandmother won't have any rolls. They were for the grandmother; now they are all gone and she won't have any!"

It seemed as if her heart would break, and Klara was alarmed.

"Heidi, Heidi, don't cry so!" she said imploringly. "I promise I will give you just as many rolls for the grandmother, or even more, when you go home, and they will be fresh and soft. The rolls you had saved were too hard to eat anyway. Come, Heidi, don't cry any more."

It was a long time before Heidi could control her sobs, but she understood Klara's comforting words.

"Will you really give me just as many rolls as I had saved for the grandmother?" she asked.

And Klara kept saying; "Yes, indeed I will, and more, too; so be happy again."

Heidi came to supper with her eyes red from weeping, and when she saw her piece of bread she had a fresh outbreak of sobbing. But this time she quickly controlled herself, for she realized that she had to behave at meals.

All through supper, when no one else was looking, Sebastian kept making strange gestures. He pointed to his own head, then to Heidi's, and winked and nodded as though trying to tell her something.

"Be comforted! I have looked after everything," he seemed to say.

Later, when Heidi went to her room and was about to get into bed, she found her little crumpled straw hat hidden under the coverlet. Sebastian had rescued it before Tinette had a chance to throw it away.

With a cry of joy, Heidi snatched up the hat and, crumpling it still more, tied it up in a handkerchief. Then she thrust it back into the darkest corner of her closet.

Chapter 9

THE MASTER OF THE HOUSE HEARS OF STRANGE DOINGS

A FEW DAYS later there was a great bustle in the Sesemann house, and hurried running up and down stairs, for the master of the house had returned. Sebastian and Tinette were bringing in one package after another from the well-laden carriage, for Herr Sesemann always brought home many beautiful things.

He went first of all to his daughter's room and greeted Klara with great tenderness. Then he reached out his hand to Heidi, who had quietly withdrawn into a corner.

"And this is our little Swiss girl, I suppose," he said kindly. "Now tell me, are you and Klara good friends? You do not quarrel and get cross, and then cry and make up, and then begin all over again?"

"No, Klara is always good to me," replied Heidi.

"And Heidi has never tried to quarrel, papa," said Klara quickly.

"That's good," said her papa as he arose. "Now you must allow me, Klärchen, to get some luncheon, for I have had nothing to eat today. Later I will come back, and you shall see what I have brought home."

Herr Sesemann went into the dining room, where Fräulein Rottenmeier, looking like a living picture of gloom, took a seat opposite his at the table.

"Fräulein Rottenmeier, what is the matter?" he asked. "Klara is very lively."

"Herr Sesemann," began the lady impressively, "we have been

frightfully deceived."

"How so?" asked Herr Sesemann, calmly sipping his coffee.

"We have decided, as you know, Herr Sesemann, to have a companion for Klara in the house. As I knew how particular you were to have only good noble associates for your daughter, I fixed my mind on a young Swiss girl, expecting to find the sort of child I had often read about—one who had sprung up in the pure mountain air, so to speak, and had gone through life without touching the earth."

"I think Swiss children must touch the earth like any others," said Herr Sesemann dryly. "Otherwise they would have wings instead of feet."

"Herr Sesemann, I am not joking," said Fräulein Rottenmeier. "We have been frightfully, really quite frightfully deceived."

"The child doesn't seem so very frightful," remarked Herr Sesemann calmly.

"You should know just *one* thing, only *one*—what sort of people and animals this creature has filled your house with in your absence. The Herr Kandidat can tell you about that."

"With animals? What am I to understand by that, Fräulein Rottenmeier?"

"This creature's whole conduct is past understanding, except from one point of view, that she has attacks of being out of her mind."

Up to this time Herr Sesemann had not taken the matter seriously. But if the Swiss child was "out of her mind," as Fräulein Rottenmeier said, this might have serious consequences for his daughter. At this moment the door opened and the Herr Kandidat came in.

"Ah, here comes our Herr Kandidat, who will give us an explanation!" exclaimed Herr Sesemann, holding out his hand. "The Herr Kandidat will drink a cup of black coffee with me,

Fräulein Rottenmeier! And now tell me, my dear sir, what is the matter with the child who has come into my house to be a companion for my daughter? What is the story about her bringing animals into the house, and what is the matter with her mind?"

The Herr Kandidat first had to express his pleasure at Herr Sesemann's safe return and bid him welcome home; but Herr Sesemann urged him to give his opinion about the matter in question. So the Herr Kandidat began:

"If I were to speak my mind about the character of this little girl, I should first make especial mention of the fact that if, on the one hand, she shows a lack of development, occasioned by a somewhat tardy instruction, on the contrary, her good qualities—"

"My dear Herr Kandidat," interrupted Herr Sesemann, "you are really giving yourself too much trouble. Tell me, has the child alarmed you by bringing in animals, and what do you think of her society for my little daughter?"

"I don't wish in any way to offend the young girl," the Herr Kandidat began again, "for if she, on the one hand, shows a certain kind of social inexperience, up to the time of her coming to Frankfurt, which coming—"

"Pray excuse me, Herr Kandidat, don't trouble yourself, I will —I will hasten to look after my daughter."

Whereupon Herr Sesemann hurried out of the room and did not return. He went into the library and sat down beside his daughter. Heidi rose from her seat.

"Look here, little girl, bring me—wait a moment—bring me—" Herr Sesemann did not exactly know what he wanted, but he wished to send Heidi away for a little while. "Bring me a glass of water."

"Fresh water?" asked Heidi.

"Yes, indeed! Quite fresh!" answered Herr Sesemann.

Heidi disappeared.

"Now, my dear Klara," said her papa, taking her hand in his, "tell me about the animals your companion brought into the house, and why Fräulein Rottenmeier should think that she is sometimes not quite right in her head?"

So Klara told her father about the turtle and the kittens, and repeated Heidi's remark which had so shocked Fräulein Rottenmeier. Herr Sesemann burst into a hearty laugh.

"So you don't care to have me send the child home, Klärchen; you are not tired of her?" he asked.

"No, no, papa; don't do that!" begged Klara. "Since Heidi has been here, something always happens every day, and the time goes so quickly; not at all as it did before she came, when nothing ever happened! Heidi tells me so many things."

"Very good, Klärchen; and here comes your little friend. Have you brought cool, fresh water?" he asked, as Heidi offered him a glass.

"Yes, fresh from the well," replied Heidi.

"Did you run to the well yourself, Heidi?" asked Klara.

"Yes, indeed; it is perfectly fresh, but I had to go a long way, for there were so many people at the first well. So I went down the street, but there were just as many people at the second well. Then I went down another street, and there I got the water. The gentleman with the white hair sent his regards to Herr Sesemann."

"So your expedition was very successful?" said Herr Sesemann, laughing. "Who is this gentleman?"

"He was passing by the well, and said, 'As you have a glass, you might give me a drink. To whom are you going to take the water?' And I said, 'To Herr Sesemann.' Then he laughed and told me to give you his regards. He had a big gold chain and a gold thing with a large red stone hanging from it, and there was a horse's head on his cane."

"That is my friend, the doctor," and "That is my old doctor," said Mr. Sesemann and Klara at the same time.

That evening, while Herr Sesemann and Fräulein Rottenmeier were sitting in the dining room, talking over household matters, he told her that his daughter's companion was to remain. He thought that the child was normal and his daughter found her society very enjoyable.

"I wish, therefore," he added very positively, "to have this child always treated kindly. Her peculiarities are not to be treated as sins. If you cannot deal with the child alone, you have the prospect of valuable assistance. My mother is coming very soon to make a long visit."

After two weeks Herr Sesemann had to leave for a business trip to Paris, but he consoled Klara by telling her that her grandmamma would soon be with her. He had hardly left when a letter arrived announcing that Frau Sesemann had started from Holstein, where she lived on an old estate. She was to arrive on the following day, and the carriage was to be sent to the railway station for her.

Klara was delighted by the news. She told Heidi so much about her grandmamma that Heidi, too, began to talk about the "grandmamma."

Fräulein Rottenmeier looked at her disapprovingly, and later that evening called the child into her room.

"You must never use the name, 'grandmamma,'" she said severely. "When you address Frau Sesemann, you are to call her 'gracious lady.' Do you understand?"

Heidi nodded. She had never heard anyone called "gracious lady," but Fräulein Rottenmeier looked so forbidding that she did not dare ask any questions.

Chapter 10

A GRANDMAMMA

~~~~~~

On the following evening there were lively preparations in
the Sesemann house, and it was plain to be seen that everyone
felt deep respect for the expected visitor. Sebastian had collected
a great number of footstools, so that the lady might find one
under her feet wherever she might sit down. Fräulein Rottenmeier, very erect, went through the rooms inspecting everything.
When the carriage rolled up to the door, Sebastian and Tinette
rushed down the stairs; Fräulein Rottenmeier in a dignified way
followed more slowly. Heidi had been told to wait in her room
until she was sent for, and she sat in a corner and repeated what
she was to say to Frau Sesemann. All the grown people she knew
were called Frau or Herr, with the name following. But she had
not dared ask Fräulein Rottenmeier for an explanation about the
strange manner of addressing the grandmamma.

She did not have long to wait before Tinette thrust her head
in at the door and told her to go to the library. As she walked
into the room, the grandmamma called in a friendly voice: "Ah,
here is the child! Come and let me look at you."

Heidi went to her and said in her clear voice, "How do you do,
Frau gracious lady."

The grandmamma laughed. "Is that what you say at home?
Did you hear that in the Alps?"

"No; no one among us has that name," answered Heidi earnestly.

"Neither has anyone here," said the grandmamma, and patted

Heidi affectionately on the cheek. "In the nursery I am grand-mamma, and you shall call me so. You can remember that, can't you?"

"Yes, I can," said Heidi confidently. "I always called you so before."

The grandmamma looked so kind that Heidi felt quite at ease. The old lady had beautiful white hair and wore a lovely lace frill around her head. Two broad strings fluttered from her cap, moving continually as though blown by a light breeze. To Heidi this seemed very peculiar.

"And what is your name, child?" asked the grandma.

"My name is only Heidi; but if anyone wants to call me Adel-heid, I pay attention." Heidi answered, just as Fräulein Rotten-meier came into the room.

"Frau Sesemann will doubtless admit," broke in Fräulein Rottenmeier, "that I had to choose a name which could be pronounced without so much difficulty."

"My dear Rottenmeier," replied Frau Sesemann, "if a person is named Heidi, and she is accustomed to the name, that is what I shall call her."

Fräulein Rottenmeier was troubled because the old lady always called her by only her last name, without any prefix. But the grandmamma usually had her own way, and there was nothing to be done about it.

The next day while Klara was taking her usual after-dinner nap, Frau Sesemann knocked on Fräulein Rottenmeier's door.

"Where does Heidi stay at this time, and what does she do?" she asked.

"She sits in her room, where she might busy herself with something useful, if she had the slightest inclination to do anything," Fräulein Rottenmeier answered. "Frau Sesemann ought to know what absurd things this creature often plans—"

"I should do the same," said Frau Sesemann, "if I had to sit alone as this child does. Bring her to my room. I want to give her some pretty books I have brought with me."

"That is just the trouble," exclaimed Fräulein Rottenmeier, wringing her hands. "What can the child do with books? In all this time she has not even learned her ABC's. It is impossible to get a single idea into this creature's head; the Herr Kandidat can tell you that!"

"She doesn't look like a child who cannot learn the alphabet," said Frau Sesemann. "Now bring her to me; she can at least look at the pictures in the books."

Fräulein Rottenmeier was about to make another remark, but Frau Sesemann had turned and was hurrying back to her own room. She was surprised to hear of Heidi's stupidity and was determined to investigate.

When Heidi came into the room, she opened her eyes wide at the sight of the gay pictures in the books on the table. The grandmamma picked up one of the books and was turning the pages when suddenly Heidi began to sob as though her heart would break. Frau Sesemann looked closely at the picture which had caused this outburst. It was of a beautiful green pasture where animals were feeding and a shepherd, leaning on a long staff, gazed at the happy creatures.

"There, there!" said the grandmamma, "I can see that this picture makes you remember something—something you miss—and that makes you sad. But, see, there is a lovely story about the picture. There are other stories in the book that can be read and repeated. Now dry your tears. We must have a little talk together."

But it was a long time before Heidi could stop sobbing. The grandmamma let her cry, merely saying now and then, "There! There! Now you are going to be happy."

Then finally, when the child was quieted, she said:

"Now you must tell me something. How do you get along in the study hours with the Herr Kandidat. Have you learned much?"

"Oh, no," Heidi sighed. "But I knew that it couldn't be learned."

"What could not be learned, Heidi? What do you mean?"

"People can't learn to read; it is too hard."

"What an idea! And where did you hear this news?"

"Peter told me so, and he knows about it. He has to keep trying, but he never can learn; it is too hard."

"Well, Peter is a strange fellow! But, you see, Heidi, you must not always take for granted what Peter tells you; you must try for yourself."

"It's of no use," said Heidi.

"Listen," said the grandmamma, "you have not learned to read yet because you believed your Peter. Now you must believe me, and I tell you, really and truly, that you can learn to read in a short time, like a great many children, who are like you and not like Peter. You have seen the shepherd in the beautiful green pasture. As soon as you can read you shall have the book for your own, so that you can learn his whole story, just as if someone told it to you. You would like that, wouldn't you, Heidi?"

"Oh, yes," said Heidi eagerly. "If I could only read now!"

"You'll learn, and it won't take long. I can see that already. But now we must look after Klara. Come, we shall take the books with us." And the grandmamma took Heidi by the hand and went into the library.

Since the day when Heidi had wanted to go home, and Fräulein Rottenmeier had told her how naughty and ungrateful she was, a change had taken place in the child. She had the idea that she could not go home if she wished, as her aunt had told her, but that she must stay in Frankfurt for a long, long time, perhaps forever. She also had understood that Herr Sesemann would think her very ungrateful, and she imagined that Klara and her grandmamma would think so, too. So Heidi dared tell no one, that she was homesick.

But in her heart the burden grew heavier and heavier. She could no longer eat; and every day she grew a little paler. At night she often lay awake for a long time thinking of the Alm. When finally she fell asleep, she would dream of the red pointed cliffs of Falkniss and the fiery snow field of Cäsaplana. In the morning she would awake, full of joy, and ready to run out of the hut, when suddenly she would remember that she was in Frankfurt. Then she would bury her head in her pillow and weep softly so no one might hear.

Heidi's unhappiness did not escape the grandmother's notice. Often, early in the morning, she could see that the child had been crying, and one day she called her into her room.

"Tell me, Heidi, what is the matter," she said kindly. "Is something grieving you?"

But Heidi did not want to seem ungrateful, for fear the kind grandmamma might not be so friendly.

"I cannot tell you," she said sadly.

"No? Can you not tell Klara?" asked the grandmamma.

"I can't tell anybody!" said Heidi, looking so unhappy that the grandmamma pitied her.

"Come, my child," she said, "I want to tell you something. When we have a sorrow we cannot speak to anybody about, then we tell the dear God in heaven, and ask him to help us. You pray every night to the dear God in heaven, don't you?"

"No, I never do that!" answered the child.

"Have you never prayed? Do you not know what it is?"

"I used to pray with the first grandmother, but it is so long ago that I have forgotten about it."

"You see, Heidi, the reason you are so sad is because you know no one who can help you. Just think what a good thing it is, when you are troubled, to tell the good Lord everything. He can always help you and make you happy again."

A glad light came into Heidi's eyes. "Can I tell Him everything?"

"Everything, Heidi, everything."

The child drew her hand out of the grandmamma's and said quickly, "May I go?"

"Certainly!" was the reply, and Heidi ran to her own room and sat down on a footstool. She folded her hands and told the dear Lord everything that was in her heart. She asked him to help her and let her go home to her grandfather.

About a week later the Herr Kandidat asked to see Frau Sesemann, as he wished to talk with her about an important matter.

"My dear Herr Kandidat, I am glad to see you!" she said, offering him her hand.

"Tell me what brings you here."

"Gracious madam," began the Herr Kandidat, "something has happened which I no longer expected. Anyone who could have seen what went before would have decided that what actually has happened was impossible—"

"Has the child Heidi possibly learned to read?" broke in Frau Sesemann.

The Herr Kandidat looked at the lady in speechless amazement.

"It is really wonderful," he said at last, "that the little girl, after all my explanations, could not learn her ABC's, and then did learn to read, almost overnight as it were. Almost equally wonderful is the gracious lady's perception in straightway suspecting that this improbable fact was possible."

"A great many wonderful things happen in the course of one's life," said Frau Sesemann, laughing with satisfaction. "Zeal in learning never does any harm, Herr Kandidat. Let us rejoice that the child has done so well, and let us hope for good progress."

She accompanied the teacher to the library, to assure herself that the delightful news was true. It was! There sat Heidi, reading a story to Klara, and with growing eagerness pushing into the new world opening up to her. People suddenly became alive and stepped out of the black letters and took part in wonderful stories.

That evening, as they were sitting down to the table, Heidi found the large book with the beautiful pictures lying by her plate. She looked inquiringly at the grandmamma.

"Yes, now it belongs to you," Frau Sesemann said.

"For always? Even when I go home?" asked Heidi, blushing with delight.

"Certainly, for always!" said the grandmamma. "Tomorrow we will begin to read it."

"But you are not going home, not for a good many years, Heidi," broke in Klara. "If grandmamma goes away, you must surely stay with me."

Before she went to sleep Heidi had to look at her beautiful book in her own room, and from that day forth she liked nothing better than to read, over and over again, the stories belonging to the lovely pictures. In the evening the grandmamma would say, "Now Heidi will read to us." This delighted the child, for the stories seemed even more beautiful when she read them aloud, and the grandmamma explained anything she did not understand.

Heidi especially liked to look at the picture of the shepherd in the green pasture. Another picture in the same story showed him after he had run away from his father's house and was obliged to tend the swine and had nothing but husks to eat. But there was still a third picture; and in this the penitent son, ragged and wasted away, was coming home, and his old father was running to welcome him with outstretched arms. This was Heidi's favorite story, and she read it over and over again, and she was never tired of hearing the explanation which the grandmamma gave.

Chapter 11

HEIDI IMPROVES IN SOME RESPECTS, AND IN OTHERS GROWS WORSE

~~~~~~

EVERY AFTERNOON, while Klara was lying down, the grandmamma called Heidi to her room where she had several pretty little dolls. She also had pieces of bright-colored materials, which she showed Heidi how to make into dresses and aprons and cloaks for the dolls; so the little girl unconsciously learned to sew. But she never looked quite happy, and there was no longer any merriment in her eyes.

"Come, my child," said Frau Sesemann one day. "Tell me why you are not happy. Have you still the same trouble in your heart?"

"Yes," said Heidi.

"Have you told the dear Lord about it?"

"Yes."

"And do you pray every day that all may be well and that He will make you happy?"

"Oh, no, I don't pray any more now."

"But why, Heidi?"

"It's of no use," Heidi answered. "When so many people in Frankfurt are praying together at night, the dear Lord cannot pay attention to them all. He has certainly not heard me."

"How do you know that, Heidi?"

"I prayed the same prayer every day for many long weeks, and the dear Lord never answered me."

"That is not so, Heidi! The dear Lord is a good Father to us all! He knows what is good for us. But if we want something

100

from him that is not good for us, he does not give it to us, but something much better, if we continue to pray to him sincerely and do not run away and lose all confidence in him.

"You see, when you forget the dear Lord and he no longer hears your voice in prayer, he forgets you, too, and lets you go whither you will. Do you want it to be so, Heidi, or will you ask the dear Lord's forgiveness for having turned away from him? If you pray every day and trust him, everything will be made right for you, and you will soon have a happy heart again."

"I will go now, right away, and ask God to forgive me," said Heidi earnestly, "and I will never forget him again."

"That is right, my child," the grandmamma replied. "Trust him, and He will help you at the right time."

It was a sad day for Heidi and Klara when Frau Sesemann left for home. After the sound of the carriage wheels had died away, the house seemed empty and still, as though everything had come to an end. Heidi came into the library, carrying her book under her arm.

"Would you like to have me read to you, Klara?" she asked her friend.

Klara was delighted with this suggestion. But Heidi had scarcely begun to read a story, which told of a dying grandmother, when she burst into sobs.

"Oh, the grandmother is dead," she cried, for to Heidi it seemed that everything she read about was actually taking place. "I can never see her again, and she has never had a single roll."

Klara tried to explain that the grandmother in the story was not the grandmother on the Alm, but Heidi was so excited she went on crying inconsolably. The thought occurred to her that the grandmother might really die, and her grandfather, too, while she was so far away. If she did not go home soon, she might find everything still and lifeless on the Alm. Then she would be all alone and never again see those who were so very dear to her.

In the meantime Fräulein Rottenmeier had come into the room. "Adelheid," she said impatiently, "we have had enough of your senseless screaming. If you ever give way to such an outburst again while you are reading, I shall take the book away from you."

Heidi turned pale, for the book was her dearest treasure. She hastily dried her tears and swallowed her sobs. This means took effect. Heidi did not cry again, no matter what she read; but sometimes she had to make such an effort to control herself that Klara said in surprise:

"Heidi, you are making the most frightful faces I have ever seen!"

The faces, however, made no sound and did not offend Fräulein Rottenmeier. But Heidi lost her appetite and was so thin and pale that Sebastian could hardly bear to look on and see how she let the nicest dishes go untouched.

"Take some of it, Mamsell," he would whisper encouragingly when he passed her something. "A good spoonful, and then another."

But his fatherly advice did no good. Heidi ate almost nothing. Then at night when she went to bed she would think of everything at home and weep into her pillow, very softly, so that no one might hear.

Thus passed the autumn and winter and spring came again. The white walls opposite her window were dazzlingly bright in the sunshine, and Heidi knew the time was drawing near for Peter to drive the goats up on the Alm again. The rock-roses would be glistening in the golden light, and every evening the mountains would be on fire.

When Heidi remembered these things, she sat down in a corner of her lonely room and put both hands over her eyes so she could not see the sunlight. She would sit without stirring, silently fighting her homesickness, until Klara called for her again.

Chapter 12

THE SESEMANN HOUSE IS HAUNTED

For several days Fräulein Rottenmeier had been acting very strangely. At dusk when she went from one room to another, she gave a quick glance behind her, as if she thought someone might be following. If she had an errand on the upper floor, she pretended there was something to carry up or down and summoned Tinette to go with her.

Tinette did exactly the same. If she had any work to do, upstairs or down, she called Sebastian, telling him she had something to carry and might not be able to manage alone. Strange to say, if Sebastian was sent to a remote part of the house, he asked Johann, the coachman, to accompany him. While this was going on upstairs, the cook, who had been in the house for many years, stood below, deep in thought among her pots and pans, and shook her head and sighed:

"That I should live to see this!"

For some time there had been something uncanny going on in the Sesemann house. Every morning when the servants came down, the big front door stood open. The first few times this happened the house was searched, but not a single thing had been stolen. Every night the door was not only double locked but a big wooden bar was put across it. But this made no difference. Every morning the door stood wide open.

At last Johann and Sebastian took courage, and prepared to spend the night in the room adjoining the great hall, to see what would happen. Fräulein Rottenmeier got out some of Herr Sesemann's weapons and gave them to Sebastian.

The two men sat down on the appointed evening, but after a while they became rather sleepy. It wasn't until the clock struck one that Johann awoke with a start.

"Now, Sebastian," he called, trying to sound brave, "we must go out and see how things are. You needn't be afraid. Come after me."

Johann opened the door and stepped into the hall. At the same moment a sharp gust of air blew in through the open front door and put out the light which Johann held in his hand. He rushed back and almost threw Sebastian, who was standing behind him, backwards into the room. In feverish haste he closed the door and turned the key. Then he pulled out his matchbox and made a light again.

Sebastian did not know just what had happened, for he had been standing behind the broad-shouldered Johann. But when he saw how pale his companion was, he cried out in fright:

"What is the matter? What was outside there?"

"The door was wide open," gasped Johann, "and there was a white form on the steps. It came up the steps, disappeared, and was gone."

Cold shivers ran down Sebastian's spine.

He and Johann sat down very close together and did not stir again until morning. Then they went out together, closed the open front door and went upstairs to tell Fräulein Rottenmeier about their experience.

That lady was quite ready to listen. When she learned what had happened, she sat down and wrote Herr Sesemann that he must come home at once. Herr Sesemann answered by return mail that he could not leave his business and that the ghost story sounded very strange to him. Probably by now Fräulein Rottenmeier's fright was a thing of the past, but if she had any more trouble he suggested that she write Frau Sesemann to come to her assistance. His mother would surely dispel the ghosts in a very short time, and never again would they venture to disturb his house.

Fräulein Rottenmeier was not pleased with the tone of this letter. She wrote immediately to Frau Sesemann and received a sarcastic reply. Frau Sesemann did not think it worth while to travel from Holstein to Frankfurt because Rottenmeier saw ghosts. A ghost had never been seen in the Sesemann house, and if there was one wandering around there now, Rottenmeier ought to be able to come to an understanding with it. If not, she should call the night watchman to her aid.

But Fräulein Rottenmeier was determined not to spend her days any longer in terror, and she knew how to help herself. She had said nothing to the children about the ghost, but now she went straight to the library, where the girls were sitting together. In a low, frightened voice she told them about the strange being that appeared every night. Klara screamed and said that she would not stay alone another moment, that her papa must come home, and Fräulein Rottenmeier must sleep in her room. Heidi ought not to be alone either.

She was so excited that Fräulein Rottenmeier promised to write to her papa at once. She offered to sleep in Klara's room, and she said that Tinette could put up a couch in Adelheid's room. But Heidi was more afraid of Tinette than of ghosts, for she had never even heard of such things, and she insisted that she would rather be alone.

After this conversation, Fräulein Rottenmeier fairly flew to her writing desk. She wrote Herr Sesemann that the mysterious goings on in the house were affecting his daughter's delicate health, and that she would not be responsible for the consequences.

This letter brought results. Two days later Herr Sesemann was standing at his door and rang so violently that Sebastian hurried downstairs two steps at a time to admit him. The master of the house did not stop to talk with the servant but went immediately to his daughter's room.

Klara greeted her papa with a cry of joy, and his stern expression softened when he saw her looking so cheerful. She assured him that she was as well as usual and that she was very grateful to the ghost, because it had caused him to hurry home.

"And what further pranks has the ghost been up to, Fräulein Rottenmeier?" asked Herr Sesemann with a smile.

"Indeed, Herr Sesemann," replied that lady, "it is no laughing matter. I have no doubt by tomorrow Herr Sesemann will find it serious enough. What is going on in this house signifies that something terrible must have happened here in days gone by and has been kept secret."

"Well, I know nothing about it," observed Herr Sesemann, "but I must beg of you not to harbor any suspicions about my honorable ancestors. Call Sebastian into the dining room; I wish to talk with him alone."

Herr Sesemann had noticed that Sebastian and Fräulein Rottenmeier were not the best of friends; so he had his suspicions.

"Come here, Sebastian," he said, when the servant entered. "Now tell me honestly, have you not been playing the part of a ghost in order to plague Fräulein Rottenmeier?"

"No, on my word. I myself have not felt at all comfortable about the matter," replied Sebastian with unmistakable frankness.

"Well, if that is the case, I will show you and the brave Johann tomorrow how ghosts look by daylight. Shame on you, Sebastian! A strong young fellow like you running away from ghosts! Go at once to my old friend, Dr. Classen; give him my compliments, and tell him he must come here without fail tonight at nine o'clock. I have come home from Paris on purpose to consult him. It is such a serious matter that he must spend the night with me. Do you understand, Sebastian?"

"Yes, indeed! Herr Sesemann may be sure that I shall do as he says."

Punctually at nine o'clock, after the children had gone to sleep and Fräulein Rottenmeier had retired, the doctor appeared. He looked somewhat anxious, but as his friend greeted him, he broke out into a hearty laugh.

"Well, well, for one who must have his doctor spend the night, you look very healthy, my friend."

"I am not your patient," replied Herr Seseman. "I called you to help me catch a ghost. The house is haunted."

The doctor laughed again.

"A fine state of affairs, doctor!" continued Herr Sesemann. "It's a shame that my friend Rottenmeier cannot enjoy it. She is convinced that a former Sesemann is wandering about here and expiating some dreadful deed."

"How did she find out about it?" asked the doctor, still very much amused.

Herr Sesemann told his friend what had happened as he led the way downstairs to the same room where Johann and Sebastian had kept watch. On the table were two lighted candelabra and two loaded revolvers. If one of the servants was trying to play a joke, a shot in the air would frighten him and give him a much-needed lesson. On the other hand, if thieves were trying to masquerade as ghosts, it would be safer to be armed.

The door into the hall was partly shut, so that the light would not frighten away the ghost. The gentlemen sat down in easy chairs and began to talk, enjoying themselves so much that the clock struck twelve before they were aware of it.

"The ghost has spied us out and is not coming tonight at all,"

said the doctor.

"Have patience, it may come at one o'clock," replied his friend.

They went on talking. The clock struck one. Everything was still; even on the street there was no sound to be heard. Suddenly the doctor lifted his finger.

"Sh, Sesemann! Don't you hear something?"

Both men listened. They heard the bar softly but quite distinctly pushed back, the key turned twice in the lock. The door opened. Herr Sesemann reached for the revolver.

"You are not afraid?" said the doctor, rising.

"It is better to be cautious," whispered Herr Sesemann seizing the candelabrum with three lighted candles in his left hand, and the revolver in his right. The doctor followed, likewise provided with lights and a revolver. They stepped into the corridor.

Through the wide-open door the pale moonlight came in and lighted up a white form, which stood motionless on the threshold.

"Who is there?" the doctor thundered, and both gentlemen, with lights and weapons, went toward the figure. It turned around and gave a little scream. There stood Heidi, with bare feet, in her white night clothes, looking bewildered at the bright lights and the firearms. She was trembling from head to foot like a little leaf in the wind.

"Child, what does this mean?" asked Herr Sesemann, in astonishment. "Why have you come down here?"

Heidi was so frightened, she could scarcely make a sound. "I don't know."

Then the doctor stepped forward. "Sesemann, the case belongs to my domain; go and sit down in your easy chair for a while. First I will take the child back where she belongs."

Whereupon he laid his revolver on the floor, took the trembling child by the hand, as a father would, and went upstairs with her.

"Don't be afraid," he said kindly. "Only be very quiet. There is no harm done."

When they were in Heidi's room, the doctor laid her in her bed and covered her up carefully. He sat down beside her and waited until she had stopped trembling. Then he took her hand and said soothingly:

"There, everything is all right. Now tell me where you wanted to go."

"I didn't want to go anywhere," said Heidi. "I did not go down there myself; I was only there all at once."

"Indeed! And did you dream anything in the night, so that you saw and heard something very clearly?"

"Yes, every night I dream, and always the same thing. I think I am with my grandfather, and I hear the fir trees roaring outdoors, and I think, 'Now the stars are sparkling in the sky,' and I run and open the door of the hut, and it is so beautiful there! But when I wake up I am in Frankfurt still." Heidi struggled to swallow the lump in her throat.

"Hm! Do you ever have any pain anywhere? In your head

or in your back?"

"Oh, no; only something presses all the time, like a great stone."

"Like something you've eaten?"

"No, not like that; but so heavy, as if I must cry hard."

"Then do you cry right out loud?"

"Oh, no, I don't dare; Fräulein Rottenmeier has forbidden that."

"Then you swallow it down till another time, don't you? You like to stay in Frankfurt, do you not?"

"Oh, yes," she replied faintly; but it sounded as if she meant the opposite.

"Where did you live with your grandfather?"

"On the Alm."

"It is not particularly pleasant there, but rather dreary, is it not?"

"Oh, no; it is so lovely there, so lovely!"

Heidi could say no more. The memories of the Alm and the excitement she had just passed through had been too much for her. She broke into loud, passionate sobbing, and the tears rushed from her eyes in streams.

"There now, cry a little," said the doctor. "It will do you good. Then go to sleep and be happy in your sleep. Tomorrow everything will be all right."

When he went downstairs, he sat down in the easy chair opposite his friend.

"Sesemann," he said, "your little protégée walks in her sleep. Unconsciously she has opened the door every night like a ghost and put all your servants into a fever of fright. In the second place, the child is wasting away from homesickness so that she is almost reduced to a little skeleton. Send her home tomorrow; that is my prescription."

Herr Sesemann rose from his chair and walked up and down the room.

"A sleepwalker!" he exclaimed. "The child sick, homesick, wasted away! All this happened in my house, and no one noticed it. Do you think, doctor, that I will send the child back to her grandfather in that condition? Take her in hand, put her under treatment. Do what you want, but make her sound and healthy. Then I will send her home, if she wants to go."

"Sesemann," replied the doctor earnestly, "her condition is no illness that can be cured with powders and pills. If you send her back now to the bracing mountain air, to which she is accustomed, she will be well again. If not—you would not like to send her back beyond all help to her grandfather, or never send her back at all, would you?"

Herr Sesemann stood still in astonishment.

"Well, if this is your advice, doctor, it must be followed immediately. Heidi shall go home tomorrow."

Chapter 13

UP THE ALM ON A SUMMER EVENING

HERR SESEMANN climbed the stairs and knocked firmly on Fräulein Rottenmeier's door. "Please hurry and come into the dining room," he called. "Preparations must be made immediately for a journey."

Fräulein Rottenmeier looked at her clock; it was half-past four in the morning. She had never risen at such an hour in her life before. Curiosity and excitement made everything she touched go wrong, and she made slow progress in dressing, for she kept hunting about uneasily in her room for the things she had already put on.

Meanwhile Herr Sesemann went the entire length of the hall and rang every one of the bells used to summon the different servants. When they came down, one after another into the dining room, they stood in surprise before the master of the house. He was walking up and down the room, looking fresh and cheerful, and not at all as if a ghost had frightened him.

Johann was immediately dispatched to put the horses and carriage in order, to be brought round later.

Tinette was ordered to waken Heidi at once, and to make her ready for a journey. Sebastian was sent to the house where Heidi's aunt was in service to bring her back.

Meanwhile Fräulein Rottenmeier had succeeded in getting dressed. Everything was all right, except her head dress which was on crooked, so from a distance she looked as if she had her face on backward. Herr Sesemann got down to business at once.

She was to procure a trunk without delay. She was to pack Heidi's things, also a good part of Klara's clothes, so that the Swiss child might have everything she needed to take home with her.

Fräulein Rottenmeier stood as if rooted to the floor, staring at Herr Sesemann. But he had no time to make further explanations and started for his daughter's room. Sitting down by Klara's bed, he told her who the ghost really was and that Heidi was in a very serious condition. If the habit of sleepwalking continued, she might some night climb upon the roof, and that would be dangerous. So he had decided to send the child home at once.

Klara was painfully surprised by this news, and at first wanted to find some way out of the difficulty. Her father remained firm in his decision, but promised to take her to Switzerland the next year, if she would be reasonable now and not grieve. So Klara yielded to what could not be helped. She asked that Heidi's trunk be packed in her room, so she might put in some special things that her friend would enjoy.

Meanwhile Aunt Dete arrived and stood waiting in the vestibule. Herr Sesemann went out to her and told her how it was with Heidi, and that he wanted her to take the child home at once, that very day. The aunt looked disappointed. She remembered the parting words of the uncle: never to come before his eyes again. Having taken the child to him, and then brought her away, it did not seem advisable to take her back again. So she did not consider the matter long but started to make excuses. It would be impossible for her to make the journey that day, the next day she would be too busy, and the day after that—

"Very well," Mr. Sesemann said curtly and dismissed her. Then he called Sebastian and told him that he was to go that very day as far as Basle with the child, and the next day he was to take her home.

"There is one thing more," he finished, "and I want you to look out for it carefully. I am acquainted at the hotel in Basle, the name of which I have written on my card for you. Show my card there and a good room will be given you for the child. Go into her room and fasten all the windows securely. When she is in bed, fasten her door on the outside, for the child wanders around in the night and might run into danger in a strange house. Do you understand?"

"Aha! That was it, was it?" exclaimed Sebastian in surprise, for a great light had just been thrown on the ghosts.

"Yes, that was it. You are a coward, and you can tell Johann that he is another," said Herr Sesemann and went to his room to write a letter to the Alm-Uncle.

Meanwhile Heidi stood waiting in her Sunday frock. Tinette had roused her from sleep, taken her clothes out of the closet and put them on hurriedly without saying a word. She never talked with the uncultivated Heidi, for she considered the child beneath her notice.

Herr Sesemann took his letter into the dining room, where breakfast was being served and asked that Heidi be called.

"Well, what do you say to it, little one?" he asked. Heidi looked at him in amazement.

"You don't know anything about it even now," Herr Sesemann laughed. "Well, you are going home today."

"Home?" repeated Heidi, hardly able to speak, and turning white as snow.

"Don't you want to know something more about it?" asked Herr Sesemann.

"Oh, yes, I do," Heidi gasped, turning red.

"Good!" said Herr Sesemann encouragingly. "Now eat a hearty breakfast. Then into the carriage you go and away."

But Heidi could not swallow a mouthful, although she tried to force herself to eat. She was in such a state of excitement that she did not know whether she was awake or dreaming.

"Sebastian must take plenty of luncheon," Herr Sesemann told Fräulein Rottenmeier. Then he turned to Heidi. "Go in to Klara until the carriage comes."

This was what Heidi wished, and she ran out of the room. In the middle of Klara's room stood a huge trunk, with the cover still wide open.

"Come!" Klara called. "See what I have packed for you."

Then she showed Heidi a number of things: dresses and aprons, underwear and sewing materials. Finally she held up a basket triumphantly. Heidi peeked inside and squealed, for there lay twelve round white rolls for the grandmother.

In their happiness the children had forgotten that the moment had come for them to part. Suddenly a call was heard: "The carriage is ready!" Then there was no time left to be sad.

Heidi ran to her room; her beautiful book from the grandmamma must still be there. No one could have packed it for she always kept it under her pillow. She laid it in the basket with the bread. She opened her closet door to see if anything had been forgotten. To be sure, there was her old red neckerchief. Heidi wrapped it around something else and laid it on top of the basket, so that the red parcel was very conspicious. Then she put on her fine hat and left her room.

The two children had to say a speedy farewell, for Herr Sesemann was waiting to take Heidi down to the carriage. Fräulein Rottenmeier stood at the head of the stairs to bid her good-by. When she noticed the strange red bundle, she took it out of the basket and threw it on the floor.

"No, Adelheid," she said, still finding fault, "you cannot leave carrying a thing like that."

Heidi did not dare to pick up her bundle again, but she looked beseechingly at the master of the house, as if she were having her greatest treasure taken from her.

"No, no," said Herr Sesemann decidedly. "The child shall carry home whatever gives her pleasure. If she takes away kittens or turtles we will not get excited about it, Fräulein Rottenmeier."

Heidi quickly picked up her bundle from the floor, her eyes beaming with gratitude and pleasure.

When Heidi reached the carriage, Herr Sesemann held out his hand and wished her a happy journey. Heidi thanked him very prettily for all his kindness.

"And I leave a thousand good-bys for the doctor," she added. "Thank him many times."

She remembered that it was the doctor who had told her the night before: "Tomorrow everything will be all right," and she thought that all her good fortune was due to him.

Soon after this, Heidi was sitting in the train, holding the basket in her lap. She would not let go of it a minute; the precious rolls for the grandmother were inside. She sat still as a mouse for several hours hardly able to realize she was really on her way home to her grandfather. She imagined how everything would look on the Alm. She thought about Peter the goatherd and the grandmother.

Suddenly she said anxiously:

"Sebastian, are you sure that the grandmother on the Alm is not dead?"

"No, no," he said soothingly. "We hope she's not dead. She must still be alive."

Heidi became absorbed again in her own thoughts, but every few minutes she peeped into the basket, for her greatest desire was to lay all the rolls on the grandmother's table.

"Sebastian," she said again, "if we could only be sure that the grandmother is still alive."

"Yes, indeed!" replied her companion, half asleep. "She's still alive; I don't see any reason why not."

After a while, Heidi's eyes also closed; and she did not awaken until Sebastian shook her by the arm.

"Wake up!" he said. "We must get out now; we are in Basle!"

On the following morning they journeyed for several hours more. Heidi again sat with the basket in her lap; on no account would she give it up to Sebastian. She did not speak, for with each hour her eagerness became more intense. Then suddenly, when she was not thinking about it, came the loud call: "Mayenfeld!" She jumped up from her seat, and in less than a minute, it seemed, she and Sebastian were standing outside with the trunk, and the train was whistling farther on up the valley.

Sebastian looked after it longingly. He did not look forward to a journey on foot, which had to end in climbing a mountain. This might be hard, and dangerous besides, in a country where everything was still half wild, as he supposed. Not far from the railway station stood a little wagon, drawn by a lean horse. Into this a broad-shouldered man was loading several large bags which had been brought by the train. Sebastian stepped up and asked him which was the safest way to Dörfli.

"All ways are safe here," was the curt reply.

Then Sebastian asked him about the best way one could go without falling over the precipices, and also how a trunk could be taken to Dörfli. The man looked at the trunk and measured it with his eyes. If it were not too heavy he would take it in his wagon, he said, since he was going that way. Finally it was arranged that the man should take both the child and the trunk, and Heidi could be sent from Dörfli up the Alm with someone that evening.

"I can go alone. I know the way from Dörfli up the Alm," said Heidi, for she had been listening attentively.

A heavy load was taken from Sebastian's mind when he found

that he would not have to climb the mountain. He beckoned Heidi to one side and handed her a heavy roll and a letter to her grandfather. He explained to her that the roll was a present from Herr Sesemann, which must be put in the bottom of her basket, under the bread. She must take good care of it, for if it were lost Herr Sesemann would be very disappointed.

"I will not lose it," said Heidi assuringly, and placed the roll and the letter in the bottom of the basket. The trunk was loaded into the wagon. Then Sebastian lifted Heidi with her basket up to the high seat and, held out his hand to bid her good-by. The driver swung himself up on the seat beside Heidi, and the wagon rolled off toward the mountain, while Sebastian, glad to escape the dreaded mountain journey, sat down in the station to wait for the returning train.

The man on the wagon was the baker of Dörfli, and he was carrying home his bags of meal. He had never seen Heidi, but like everyone else in Dörfli he knew about the child that had been brought to the Alm-Uncle. Besides, he had known Heidi's parents and he wondered if this was the much-talked-of little girl.

"You are the child who was up with the Alm-Uncle, your grandfather, aren't you?" he asked.

"Yes."

"Did you fare badly? Is that why you have come home from so far?"

"No one could fare better than I did in Frankfurt," said Heidi.

"Why are you running home then?"

"Only because Herr Sesemann allowed me, or I should not be coming home."

"Bah! Why didn't you prefer to stay there, if you were only *allowed* to come home?"

"Because I would a thousand times rather be at home with my grandfather on the Alm than anywhere else in the world."

"Perhaps you'll think differently when you get up there," growled the baker.

Then he began to whistle and said nothing more. Heidi looked around her, trembling with excitement as she recognized familiar landmarks. In the distance she could see the lofty peaks of the Falkniss mountain looking down at her, and they seemed to be greeting her like good old friends. As they came into Dörfli, the clock was just striking five. In a moment a crowd of women and children gathered around the wagon.

"Thank you," said Heidi, when the baker lifted her from the cart. "My grandfather will come for my trunk."

She tried to run away, but people began asking her questions on every side. Heidi pressed through the crowd with such anxiety on her face that they reluctantly made room for her and let her pass.

"You see how frightened she is; she has every reason to be," they said.

Then they began to tell one another how the Alm-Uncle was worse than ever, and would not speak a word to anyone. If the child had any sense, she would not run to the old dragon's nest. Here the baker interrupted to tell about the gentleman who had brought the child as far as Mayenfeld and parted from her in a very friendly manner. He had paid the fare the baker asked, without any bargaining, and given him an extra fee besides. Heidi had said she had been well off where she was but was anxious to come back to her grandfather. This news caused great surprise and was immediately spread through all Dörfli.

Heidi ran up the mountain as fast as she could go, but now and then she had to stop to get her breath. The basket on her arm was heavy, and the path grew steeper and steeper. She had only one thought:

"Will the grandmother be sitting in the corner at her spinning wheel? Or has she died while I was away?"

Soon Heidi saw the hut in the hollow on the Alm, and her heart began to throb. She ran still faster; her heart beat louder and louder. By the time she reached the hut she was trembling so that she could hardly open the door. She ran into the room and stood there a moment, unable to speak, completely out of breath.

"Our Heidi used to run in like that," came a voice from the corner. "Ah, if I could only see the child once more! Who has come in?"

"Here I am, grandmother; here I am, really!" exclaimed Heidi.

Rushing into the corner she threw herself on her knees before the grandmother. The old lady stroked the child's curly hair but was so overjoyed that at first she could not speak.

"Is it really you, child?" she said at last. "Are you really here?" And two tears dropped from her blind eyes on Heidi's hand.

"Yes, really, grandmother," said Heidi. "Do not cry. I will come to see you every day and never go away again. You won't have to eat hard bread for many days, for see what I have brought you."

Heidi took one roll after another out of her basket, until she had piled all twelve in the grandmother's lap.

"Oh, child! What a blessing you have brought me!" exclaimed the grandmother. "But the greatest blessing is you yourself." Then she stroked the child's curly hair.

Just then Peter's mother came in. "Why, it is Heidi," she exclaimed in astonishment. "How can it be possible?"

Heidi rose and shook hands with Brigitte, who continued to stare at the child.

"You should see what a beautiful dress she is wearing, mother," she said. "Does that hat trimmed with feathers, on the table, belong to you, Heidi? Just put it on, so I can see how you look in it."

"No, I will not," said Heidi decidedly. "You can have it. I don't need it any longer. I still have my own."

Whereupon Heidi opened her little red bundle and took out her old hat. She had never forgotten how, when she was leaving her grandfather, he had called after her that he never wanted to see her in a hat trimmed with feathers. That was why she had kept her own hat so carefully, for she had always hoped for the time when she could go home to him.

At first Brigitte refused to take the hat, but Heidi was firm. She laid it in the corner behind the grandmother. Then she took off her lovely dress and folded the red neckerchief over her underwaist.

"Now I must go home to my grandfather, but tomorrow I will

come again. Good night, grandmother."

"Yes, come again, Heidi; come again tomorrow morning," said the grandmother, as she pressed Heidi's hand.

"Why have you taken off your beautiful dress?" asked Brigitte.

"Because I would rather go to my grandfather without it. He might not know me. You hardly knew me in it."

Brigitte followed Heidi to the door "You must take care of yourself," she whispered. "Peterli says the Alm-Uncle is always very cross now and never says a word."

Heidi only said, "good night," and went on up the mountain with her basket on her arm. The evening sun shone on the green Alm, and soon the snow field on Cäsaplana came into sight and gleamed in the distance.

Every few steps Heidi had to stand still and look about her. A red glow fell on the grass at her feet. She turned around and the rocky peaks on Falkniss seemed to be in flames. The broad snow field was aglow, and rosy clouds were drifting overhead. Down below, the valley swam in a golden vapor.

The child stood in the midst of all this glory, tears of joy running down her cheeks. She had to fold her hands, and, looking up to Heaven, thank the dear Lord aloud that he had brought her back home and that everything was even more beautiful than she had remembered.

Not until the light began to fade could she move away from the place. Then she ran so fast up the mountain that it was not long before she saw the boughs of the fir trees above the roof, and then the roof itself, and then the whole hut. On the seat beside it sat her grandfather, smoking his pipe, and over the hut the old fir trees were rocking and roaring in the evening wind. Heidi ran all the faster, and before the Alm-Uncle could really see who was coming she threw her basket on the ground and hugged him. In her excitement at seeing him again she was unable to say anything, except to keep exclaiming: "Grandfather! Grandfather! Grandfather!"

Neither did the grandfather say anything. For the first time in many years his eyes grew moist. He loosened Heidi's arms from his neck and took her on his knee.

"So you have come home again," he said. "You don't look very well. Did they send you away?"

"Oh, no," Heidi answered. "Klara and the grandmamma and Herr Sesemann were all so good to me. But, you see, grandfather, I could hardly wait to come home again to you. Sometimes I thought I would choke, but I never said anything because that would have been ungrateful.

"Then suddenly one morning Herr Sesemann called me very early. I believe the doctor was the cause of it, but perhaps it tells about it in the letter—"

She jumped down, took the letter and her roll out of her basket and laid them in her grandfather's hand.

"This belongs to you," he said laying the roll on the seat beside him. He read the letter slowly and put it his pocket without saying a word.

"Do you think you can drink milk with me still, Heidi?" he asked, taking the child by the hand and leading her into the hut. "Bring your money with you. You can buy a bed with it, and clothes enough to last you for two or three years."

"I really don't need it, grandfather," said Heidi. "I have a bed already, and Klara packed so many clothes for me that I shall never need any more."

"Then we'll put the money in the cupboard. You'll be able to use it some time."

Heidi was delighted to see the inside of the hut again. She looked in every corner and climbed up the ladder.

"Oh, grandfather," she called down, somewhat concerned, "my

bed is gone."

"You will soon have another," sounded from below. "I didn't know that you would return. Now come and get your milk!"

Heidi came down and took her seat on her high stool in the old place. She grasped her little bowl and drank as eagerly as if she had never tasted anything so delicious.

"There is nothing in all the world so good as our milk," she said, taking a deep breath.

A shrill whistle sounded outside. Heidi shot out of the door like lightning. There was the whole flock of goats, skipping, jumping, and leaping down from the heights above, with Peter in their midst. When he saw Heidi he stood perfectly still, as if rooted to the spot.

Heidi called, "Good evening, Peter!" and rushed in among the goats. "Schwänli! Bärli! Do you know me still?"

The goats must have recognized her voice, for they rubbed their heads against her and began to bleat. Heidi called them by name, one after the other, and they ran like wild creatures in confusion and crowded around her. She threw her arms around the affectionate Schneehöpli, stroked the violent Distelfinck, and was pushed and jolted hither and thither by the fond, trusting little animals.

Finally she thrust them aside and held out her hand to Peter. "Aren't you going to say good evening to me?" she asked.

"Are you back again?" the astonished Peter managed to say at last. "Will you come with me again tomorrow?"

"No, not tomorrow, but the day after, perhaps. Tomorrow I must go to the grandmother's."

"It is good to have you back," said Peter.

He started homeward, but never before had he had so much trouble with his goats. Heidi had walked away with one arm around Schwänli's and the other about Bärli's neck, when all the others turned and ran after the three. Heidi had to go into the shed with her two goats and shut the door, or Peter would never have succeeded in getting on with his flock.

When the child came back into the hut, she found her bed made up again, wonderfully high and fragrant, for the hay had not been in long. The grandfather had carefully spread the clean linen sheet over it. Heidi lay down and had a refreshing sleep, such as she had not enjoyed for a whole year. During the night her grandfather left his couch at least ten times, climbed the ladder and listened carefully to make sure that she was not restless.

But Heidi slept on and wandered about no longer, for her great longing was satisfied. She had seen the mountains and cliffs in the evening glow and she had heard the fir trees roaring. She was at home again on the Alm.

Chapter 14

SUNDAY WHEN THE CHURCH BELLS RING

HEIDI STOOD under the swaying branches of the fir trees, waiting for her grandfather who was going to fetch the trunk from Dörfli while she stayed with the grandmother. The child could hardly wait to see the grandmother again, yet the time did not seem long. She could not listen enough to the rustle of the fir trees and drink in the beauty of the green pastures with their golden blossoms.

The grandfather came out of the hut, and they went down the path together. At Peter's hut they parted and Heidi ran in. The grandmother had heard her step, and called out to her affectionately:

"Have you come, child? Have you come again?"

She grasped Heidi's hand and held it tightly, as though she feared the child might be taken away again. She talked about the rolls and how good they had tasted. Then Brigitte added that the grandmother had eaten only one roll the day before, because she was afraid they would soon be gone. Heidi listened attentively to Brigitte and thought for some time.

"I know what I will do," said Heidi. "I will write a letter to Klara, and she will send me many more rolls. I had a great pile just like them in my closet, and when they were taken away from me Klara said she would give me just as many more and she will do so."

"Dear me!" said Brigitte. "That is a good idea; but think, they would grow hard, too. If we only had a spare penny now and then, the baker down in Dörfli makes them. But I am hardly able to pay for the black bread."

A joyful light spread over Heidi's face.

"Oh, I have a tremendous lot of money, grandmother!" she exclaimed triumphantly. "Now I know what I can do with it. Every single day you must have a new roll, and two on Sunday, and Peter can bring them up from Dörfli."

"No, no, child!" said the grandmother in disapproval. "The money was not given you for that. You must give it to your grandfather, and he will tell you what to do with it."

But Heidi would not listen. She shouted and danced around the room and exclaimed again and again:

"Now the grandmother can eat a roll every day and will grow quite strong again, and—oh, grandmother!" She stopped suddenly, for she had spied the old hymn book on the shelf and a new thought came to her.

"Grandmother, I can read quite well now. Shall I read a song out of your old book?"

"Oh, yes!" said the grandmother. "Can you really read, child?"

Heidi climbed up in a chair and took down the book, covered thick with dust. She wiped it clean, sat down on her stool beside the grandmother, and asked what she should read.

"Whatever you like, child," said the grandmother and waited with eager expectancy.

Heidi turned the leaves and read a line here and there.

"Here is something about the sun; I will read you that," she said.

> *"The sun o'erflowing*
> *With splendor glowing,*
> *From golden fountains*
> *Pours o'er our mountains*
> *A spirit-quickening glory of light.*

Below I wandered
And, mournful, pondered,
But now arising
With change surprising
I turn to the sky my enraptured sight.

Mine eye beholdeth
What God unfoldeth
To tell the story
Of boundless glory—
How vast the sum of his infinite might!

Behind those portals
Henceforth immortals,
Our friends arisen
From fleshly prison
Have entered the realms of boundless delight.

His grace unbounded
In love is founded;
The humblest creature
May share His nature—
The lowest depth and the highest height.

Today we languish
In grief and anguish,
But earthly sorrow
Shall fade tomorrow
After the storm the sun shines bright."

The grandmother sat still with folded hands and an expression
of indescribable joy on her face, such as Heidi had never seen

there before, although the tears were running down her cheeks. When Heidi stopped reading she said entreatingly:

"Oh, just once more, Heidi, let me hear it just once more!"

The child began again:

> *"Today we languish*
> *In grief and anguish,*
> *But earthly sorrow*
> *Shall fade tomorrow*
> *After the storm the sun shines bright.*
>
> *Sweet peace and pleasure*
> *In boundless measure*
> *We know is given*
> *In the gardens of heaven;*
> *And thither my hopes yearn day and night!"*

"Heidi, that gives me light! It gives me light in my heart. Oh, how much good you have done me!"

The grandmother repeated the joyful words again and again; and Heidi beamed with pleasure. Then someone knocked on the window, and she saw her grandfather outside, beckoning to her to go home with him. She got up quickly, but not without assuring the grandmother that she would come again the next day.

Brigitte ran after Heidi with her dress and hat so she might take them with her. Heidi took the dress on her arm, for her grandfather knew her now, she thought; but the hat she obstinately refused. Brigitte must keep it, for Heidi was determined never, never to put it on her head again.

On the way home Heidi had much to tell her grandfather: how happy the grandmother had looked when she heard the words of the old hymns and how they could get white bread for her down in Dörfli, if they only had the money.

"Even if the grandmother is not willing, you'll give me my money, won't you, grandfather?" said Heidi. "Then I can give Peter a coin to buy a roll every day and two on Sunday."

"But the bed, Heidi?" said the grandfather. "A real bed would be a good thing for you. There would be enough left for many rolls."

But Heidi gave him no peace. She assured him that she slept much better on her bed of hay than she had ever done in her pillowed bed in Frankfurt. She begged so hard that he finally said:

"The money is yours; do whatever pleases you. You can get bread for the grandmother with it for many a long year."

Heidi shouted for joy. "Hurrah! Now the grandmother will never have to eat hard black bread any more. Oh, grandfather, everything is lovelier than it ever was before in our lives!"

Heidi jumped up and down; then suddenly she became very serious. Taking her grandfather's hand, she said:

"If the dear Lord had done right away what I prayed for so hard, everything would not be as it is now. I would only have come home again and brought the grandmother just a few rolls, and I couldn't have read to her. But the dear Lord had thought it all out so much better than I knew. I am glad that he did not grant what I asked and longed for! Now I will always pray as the grandmamma told me; and if the dear Lord does not do as I ask, I will remember it is because he is planning something much better, just the way he did when I was in Frankfurt. We will pray every day, won't we, grandfather? We will never forget him."

"And if one should do so?" murmured the grandfather.

"Oh, it would not be well for him, for then the dear Lord would

forget him, too."

"That is true, Heidi; how did you know it?"

"From the grandmamma; she told me all about it."

The grandfather was silent for a while. Then he said, "And if it is so, then it is so. No one can go back, for whomever God has forgotten, he has forgotten."

"Oh, no, grandfather; one can go back. That I know, too, from the grandmamma. And then it says so in the beautiful story in my book. When we get home, you shall see how beautiful the story is."

As soon as they reached the hut, Heidi ran inside to get her book. With one bound she was by her grandfather's side and had

found her story, for she had read it so often that the book opened
of itself at the place. Heidi read with great feeling about the
Prodigal Son.

"Isn't that a beautiful story, grandfather?" she asked.

"Yes, Heidi, the story is beautiful," he said, but his face was
so serious that Heidi became quite still and looked at her pictures. She quietly pushed the book in front of her grandfather.
"See how happy he is!" she said, pointing to the picture of the
prodigal son's return home, in which he stands in fresh garments
beside his father, and once more is his son.

A few hours later, when Heidi was asleep, her grandfather
climbed the little ladder. He put his lamp beside her bed so
that the light fell on the sleeping child. She lay there with folded
hands, for she had not forgotten to pray. He stood looking at
her for a long time. Then he, too, folded his hands and bowed
his head.

"Father," he prayed, "I have sinned against Heaven and before
Thee and am no more worthy to be called Thy son!" And great
tears rolled down his cheeks.

In the early daylight the Alm-Uncle stood in front of his hut,
looking around with beaming eyes. The sound of early bells
came up from below, and the birds in the fir trees were beginning their morning songs. He stepped back into the hut.

"Come, Heidi!" he called. "The sun is up! Put on a good dress,
and we will go to church together!"

Heidi was delighted at this request, and it did not take her
long to get ready. In a short time she climbed down the ladder
wearing her fine Frankfurt dress, but she remained standing in
front of her grandfather and looked at him in surprise.

"Oh, grandfather, I have never seen you look so before!" she
exclaimed. "You have never worn the coat with the silver but-
tons. You are so splendid in your beautiful Sunday coat!"

The old man looked at the child with a contented smile, "And you in yours; now come!" he said.

He took Heidi's hand in his, and they went together down the mountain. The clear-toned bells were sounding in every direction. "Do you hear them, grandfather?" asked Heidi. "It is like a great festival."

Down in Dörfli the people were already in church and just beginning to sing when the grandfather and Heidi entered and sat down in the last row. But in the midst of the singing the person sitting next them nudged his neighbor with his elbow and said:

"Have you noticed? The Alm-Uncle is in church!"

This person nudged the next one and so on, and in a short time it was being whispered in every corner: "The Alm-Uncle! The Alm-Uncle!" and nearly everyone turned to look.

But when the pastor began to preach they became attentive. There was such warm praise and thanksgiving in the pastor's words that his listeners felt that something wonderful had happened. When the service was over, the Alm-Uncle went out, holding the child by the hand, and walked to the parsonage. The other people stood in little groups outside the church, talking excitedly.

"It may be the Alm-Uncle is not so bad as they say," said one man. "Did you notice how carefully he held the little one by the hand?"

"That is what I have always thought," said another. "Brigitte has told us how kind the Alm-Uncle has been to the grandmother."

Then the baker said, "Wasn't I the first to tell you? Do you suppose a child would leave a fine home to go back to a grandfather if he was wicked and she was afraid of him?"

As the people talked, they began to feel more kindly toward

the Alm-Uncle. Suddenly it seemed as if they were waiting to welcome an old friend who had long been absent.

Meanwhile the Alm-Uncle had gone to the study door and knocked. The pastor opened it and met the visitor, not with surprise, as he might have done, but as if he were expecting him. He grasped the old man's hand and shook it heartily. The Alm-Uncle stood in silence, for he was not prepared for such a warm greeting. Then he collected himself and said:

"I have come to ask the pastor to forget the words I said to him on the Alm, and that he will not bear me ill will for being obstinate toward his well-meant advice. The pastor was right, and I was wrong. I will follow his advice, and next winter take up quarters in Dörfli, for the severe weather up yonder is not good for the child; she is too delicate. Even if the people down here look at me askance, I deserve nothing better, and certainly the pastor will not do so."

The pastor's friendly eyes beamed with delight. "Neighbor," he said, "I promise that you shall never regret your willingness to come down and live among us again. You will always be welcome in my house as a dear friend and neighbor, and we shall find good friends also for the little girl."

The pastor laid his hand on Heidi's curly head, then took her by the hand and led her to the door. The people standing around outside saw him shake hands with the Alm-Uncle, as if they were close friends.

Scarcely had the door closed behind the pastor, when the whole assembly pressed toward the Alm-Uncle, and so many hands were held out to him that he did not know which he ought to grasp first.

"I am glad, uncle," said one. "I am glad, uncle, that you are coming back to us again!"

And another said, "I have long wanted to speak with you!"

Similar remarks were heard on every side, and when the uncle told them that he intended to take up his quarters in Dörfli again and spend the winter with his old acquaintances, there was great rejoicing. A number of the villagers walked with the grandfather and child part of the way up the Alm, and when they left, they made him promise to call on them when he came down again.

Heidi looked at him in surprise. "Grandfather, you have never looked so handsome before."

"Do you think so?" He smiled. "Well, you see, Heidi, I feel happy because I am on good terms with people and at peace with God and man; that does one good! The dear Lord was good to me when he sent you up on the Alm."

When they reached Peter the goatherd's hut the grandfather opened the door and went in.

"Good day, grandmother," he called. "I think we must do a little more mending before the autumn wind comes."

"Dear me, that is the uncle!" exclaimed the grandmother. "That I should live to see this! I can thank you for all you have done for us, uncle! May God reward you for it!"

The grandmother held out her hand and the uncle shook it heartily. "I have one thing more to ask of you," she said, her voice trembling. "Do not let Heidi go away again before I lie at rest in the churchyard. You do not know what the child is to me."

"Never fear, grandmother," said the uncle soothingly. "We shall all stay together, God willing, for a long time."

Then Brigitte drew the uncle mysteriously into a corner and showed him the lovely hat trimmed with feathers. She told him that she did not like to take such a fine gift from a child.

But the grandfather looked well-pleased at Heidi and said, "The hat is hers, and if she doesn't care to wear it any more it is all right. If she gave it to you, why, take it."

Brigitte was delighted at this unexpected decision. "It is really worth more than ten francs," she said, and in her delight she held the hat high in the air. "What a blessing this Heidi has brought home with her from Frankfurt!"

Just then Peter came in. Panting and out of breath, he stood in the middle of the floor and held out a letter for Heidi. The postmaster in Dörfli had given it to him. Then everyone sat down around the table and listened eagerly while Heidi read the letter aloud.

It was from Klara Sesemann, who wrote how lonely she had been. She had begged so hard to visit Heidi that her father had consented to take her and the grandmamma on a journey to Ragatz the coming autumn. The grandmamma sent word that she thought Heidi had done right in wishing to buy the grandmamma some rolls, and she was sending the old lady some coffee to drink with them.

Everyone was so excited at the prospect of Klara's visit and there was so much to talk about that even the grandfather did not notice how late it was getting.

"But the best thing that happened," said the grandmother, "was for an old friend to come and give us his hand again, just as he used to do long ago. You will come again soon, uncle, and send the child tomorrow."

The grandfather promised, and then it was time to go. As he and Heidi walked home they could hear the peaceful sound of the evening bells ringing down in the valley, and the whole Alm seemed to shine in the Sunday evening light.

HEIDI

PART II

Chapter 1

PREPARATIONS FOR A JOURNEY

THE KIND doctor, who had decided that Heidi must be taken back to her mountain home, was passing along the broad street toward the Sesemann house. It was a sunny September morning, but he was gazing at the white stones at his feet and did not notice the blue sky. The doctor's only daughter had been taken from him by death a few months before, and there was a sadness in his face that had not been there in the spring.

When he rang the Sesemann bell, Sebastian opened the door. "Good morning, Sebastian," said the doctor in his usual friendly voice and went up the stairs.

"I am glad you have come, doctor," called Mr. Sesemann. "I want to talk to you again about Klara's going to Switzerland."

"My dear Sesemann, it can't be," replied the doctor, taking a seat beside his friend. "This is the third time you have sent for me, although I keep telling you the same thing."

"Yes, you are right." Mr. Sesemann laid his hand entreatingly on the doctor's shoulder. "But it is hard for me to deny the child the trip I promised her. She has borne these last bad days so patiently in the hope that she would be able to visit her friend, Heidi, in the Alps."

"I know," said the doctor, "but Klara has not had such a bad summer in years. She could not take such a long journey without grave danger. If there is to be any hope for her recovery, we must use the greatest care and the most cautious treatment. She shall go next spring if she is better."

Herr Sesemann, who had listened silently and with an expression of sad submission, sprang to his feet.

"Doctor, tell me honestly," he said, "have you really any hope for her improvement?"

The doctor shrugged his shoulders.

"Little," he said in a low voice. "But think for me, friend! Have you not a dear child who longs for you when you are away, and is delighted when you come home? Although she has to be deprived of much that others enjoy, she is, in some respects, highly favored. You are fortunate to be together; think of my lonely house!"

Herr Sesemann began to stride up and down the room, as he was in the habit of doing when deeply absorbed in any matter. Suddenly he stood still in front of his friend.

"Doctor, I have an idea. I cannot see you like this. You must get out of yourself a little; and do you know how? You shall undertake the journey and visit the child Heidi in our place."

The doctor was surprised at this proposal, but Herr Sesemann gave him no time to object. He seized his friend by the arm and led him to his daughter's room. Klara always looked forward to seeing the doctor, and she looked up at him with a wan smile when he sat down beside her bed.

Herr Sesemann moved up his chair, and, taking Klara's hand, began to talk about the journey to Switzerland. He glided quickly over the fact that it was now out of the question, for he was afraid of the tears that would be sure to come. He then passed on to the new plan and impressed Klara with the fact that her dear friend would derive great benefit by taking this journey.

The tears indeed came and swam in Klara's blue eyes, although she tried her best to keep them back. She knew how her papa disliked to see her cry, but the prospect of this visit to Heidi had been her only comfort during the long, lonely sum-

mer. But Klara was not in the habit of arguing. She knew her papa was denying her the trip for her own good. She choked down her sobs and seized the doctor's hand.

"Oh, please, you will go, won't you?" she begged. "Then come back and tell me about everything up on the Alm. I want to know what Heidi is doing and all about her grandfather and Peter and the goats. Then you must take some presents from me to Heidi. I have something for the grandmother, too. Please, doctor, do go; and while you are gone I will truly take all the cod-liver oil you prescribe."

Whether this promise decided the matter or not, the doctor smiled and said:

"Then I must certainly go, Klärchen, for you will grow round and strong as papa and I would like to have you. When must I start? Have you decided that, too?"

"Certainly; tomorrow early," replied Klara.

"Yes, she is right," said her father. "The sun is shining, the sky is blue, and no time is to be lost, for it is a shame not to be enjoying such a day in the Alps."

The doctor had to laugh.

"Next thing you will be reproaching me for not being there already, Sesemann, so I shall do well to get away."

But Klara held the doctor fast; she had first to give him all sorts of messages for Heidi and to remind him of so many things which he must notice and then tell her about. The things she wished to send to Heidi would be taken to him later, for Fräulein Rottenmeier would have to help pack them.

Servants often have a wonderful faculty of finding out, long before they have been told, what is going on in their master's house. When Sebastian opened the front door for the doctor, he made a deep bow and said with his usual politeness, "Will you be so kind as to give the little Mamsell my regards?"

"Why, Sebastian," said the doctor pleasantly, "do you know so soon that I am going away?"

Sebastian was obliged to cough.

"I am—I have—I don't know certainly—oh, yes, I remember, as I happened to be passing through the hall just now I heard the little Mamsell's name mentioned. It often happens that we put one thought and another together, and so—and in that way—"

"Yes, indeed!" said the doctor, laughing. "And the more thoughts one has, the more one knows. Good-by, Sebastian, I will deliver your message."

Klara expected to have a struggle with Fräulein Rottenmeier before she would consent to send away all the things that Klara wanted Heidi to have. But this time she was happily disappointed; Fräulein Rottenmeier was unusually good-natured. She laid out the articles Klara selected on a large table. But packing these was no easy task, for the presents were of such different shapes. First, there was a thick cloak with a hood for

Heidi, so that during the coming winter she might visit the grandmother whenever she liked and not have to wrap up in a heavy sack.

Next came a warm shawl and a box of cookies for the old grandmother. A huge sausage followed. Klara had first intended this for Peter, because he never had anything to eat but bread and cheese. But she changed her mind, fearing that Peter, in his delight, might want to eat the whole sausage at once. So it was decided that his mother, Brigitte, was to have it first and take a good share of it for herself and the grandmother. Then she was to give Peter his portion at different times.

There also was a little bag of tobacco for the grandfather who liked to smoke his pipe when he sat in front of the hut in the evening. Last came a number of mysterious little bags, packages, and boxes, which Klara had taken special delight in collecting, for they contained all kinds of surprises to give Heidi pleasure.

At last the work was finished, and an imposing package lay on the floor, ready for the journey. Just looking at it made Klara happy. She knew exactly how Heidi would jump up and down and shout with joy when the huge bundle reached her.

Then Sebastian came in and swung the bundle up on his shoulder to take it to the doctor's house.

Chapter 2

A GUEST ON THE ALM

THE MOUNTAINS were glowing in the early dawn, and the wind was blowing through the fir trees and rocking their old branches vigorously to and fro. Heidi opened her eyes; the sound had awakened her. She loved this rushing sound and could hardly wait to go outside. She jumped from her bed and dressed hurriedly.

When she came down the ladder, her grandfather's couch was empty. She ran outdoors. There he stood in front of the hut, gazing up at the sky, as he did every morning to see what kind of a day it was going to be.

Rosy clouds floated above, and the sky grew bluer and bluer, and the heights and the pasture land seemed flooded with gold, for the sun was just rising above the lofty cliffs.

"Oh, how beautiful! Good morning, grandfather," Heidi called.

"Well, are your eyes already opened?" said the grandfather.

Then Heidi ran under the fir trees and danced under the swaying boughs. The wind rushed and roared in the treetops, and she shouted with joy.

Meanwhile the grandfather had gone to the shed and had milked Schwänli and Bärli. He brushed and washed them for their journey up the mountain, and brought them outside. When Heidi saw her friends, she ran to them and threw her arms about their necks, and they bleated trustfully. As though anxious to give proof of their affection, they pressed closer and closer to her shoulders, so that she was almost crushed between them.

But Heidi was not afraid, and when the lively Bärli butted and pushed too hard, she said, "No, Bärli, you push like the big Türk," and Bärli drew back her head and retreated to a proper distance. Then Schwänli stretched up her head and bleated in a superior way, as much as to say, "No one shall think of me that I behave like the Türk." For the snow-white Schwänli was more dignified than Bärli.

Peter's whistle sounded from below, and soon all the other lively goats came leaping up the mountain, the nimble Distel-finck bounded ahead of the others. Heidi ran into the midst of the flock, which jostled her hither and thither with loud, affectionate greetings.

"You can come with me again today," said Peter peevishly.

"No, I can't, Peter," Heidi replied. "My friends may come from Frankfurt at any moment now, and I must be at home."

"You have said that a good many times already," growled Peter.

"But it is still true, and it will be true until they come," replied Heidi. "Don't you know that I must be at home when they are coming from Frankfurt to see me?"

The grandfather's deep voice sounded from the hut:

"Why doesn't the army move forward? Is it the fault of the field marshal or the troops?"

In a twinkling Peter wheeled around and swung his rod in the air, making it whistle. The goats, knowing the sound well, started at full speed up the mountain, with Peter behind them.

Every morning Heidi tried to make her bed, smoothing it until it looked quite even. Then she ran about the hut, placing every chair in its place, and if anything was lying or hanging about, she put it tidily into the closet. She took a cloth, climbed up on a stool, and rubbed the table until it was perfectly clean. When her grandfather came in again, he would look around him with satisfaction and say:

"Now, it is always like Sunday here; Heidi did not go away for nothing."

Today also, after Peter had gone, Heidi set about her work. But it was such a lovely morning that in a few minutes she ran outdoors to look up at the sky and listen to the wind roaring through the fir trees. The Alm-Uncle was busy in the shop when he heard her call:

"Grandfather! Grandfather! Come!"

He hurried out, afraid that something might have happened to the child. Then he saw her running toward the cliff, screaming:

"They are coming! They are coming, and the doctor first of all!"

Heidi rushed to meet her friend. He held out his hand to greet her.

"How do you do, doctor! Thank you a thousand times."

"Good morning, Heidi," he said, smiling. "But why do you thank me?"

"Because you helped me to come home," she said.

The doctor's face lighted. He had not expected such a reception in the Alps. He had supposed that the child Heidi would hardly remember him. Also he was bringing her disappointing news, and he was afraid he might not be welcome.

"But where are Klara and the grandmamma?" she asked.

"I have to tell you something that will pain you as well as myself," replied the doctor. "You see, Heidi, I have come alone. Klara has been very ill and was not able to take the journey; so the grandmamma did not come either. But in the spring, when the days are warm and long again, then they will surely come."

At first Heidi said nothing. She looked up at the doctor, as though bewildered by her disappointment. Then she noticed the sad expression in his eyes, and she thought perhaps he was worrying because Klara and the grandmamma had been unable

to come.

"Never mind!" she said consolingly, for Heidi could not bear to have anyone look sad. "Spring will soon be here. Now we will go up to my grandfather."

Hand in hand with her good friend, she climbed up to the hut. The Alm-Uncle had heard so much about the doctor he felt as though he already knew Heidi's friend, and he held out his hand in welcome.

Then the two men sat down on the bench before the hut, making a place for Heidi between them. The doctor whispered that a big package, which he had brought from Frankfurt for her, would soon be carried up the mountain, and that it would give her greater pleasure than the old doctor could. Heidi was very curious to know what this might be.

The grandfather urged his new friend to spend the beautiful autumn days on the Alm. So the doctor decided, instead of going as far away as Ragatz, to take a room at the inn in Dörfli and come up on the mountain every morning.

Meanwhile the sun had announced that it was midday. The Alm-Uncle went into the hut, but immediately came out again, bringing a table, which he placed in front of the bench.

"There, Heidi, now bring out what we need to eat," he said. "The gentleman will have to make the best of it, for if our cooking is plain, our dining room is all that could be desired."

"I think so, too," replied the doctor as he gazed down into the valley bathed in sunlight, "and I accept your invitation. Everything must taste good up here."

Heidi ran back and forth, setting the table, while the grandfather prepared the meal. He came out with a steaming jug of milk and the golden toasted cheese. He cut thin, delicious slices of rosy meat, which he had dried in the pure mountain air. The doctor declared that he had never before eaten such a delicious meal.

"Yes, indeed, our Klara must come here," he said. "She would gain strength, and if she should have such an appetite as I have today, she would become plump and robust as she never has been in all her life."

Then someone came climbing up from below with a big package on his back.

"Ah, here is what I brought from Frankfurt," said the doctor, rising and drawing Heidi with him. "Come, child! Help me open it."

Heidi's eyes grew big with astonishment when the doctor lifted the lid of the box. Then she screamed with delight:

"Oh, see, the nice cakes Klara sent for the grandmother to eat

with her coffee! And here's a big sausage and a warm shawl and other presents, too!"

Heidi wanted to gather the things together and hurry down to the grandmother's at once, but her grandfather promised that she could go later when the doctor went down into the valley. Then Heidi found the bag of tobacco, and the Alm-Uncle was pleased. He immediately filled his pipe, and the two men sat on the bench talking, while Heidi ran back and forth examining her treasures.

Suddenly she came back to the bench and looked up at her guest.

"No, nothing has given me more pleasure than the old doctor has," she said.

The doctor laughed and said that he wouldn't have thought it.

When the sun went down behind the mountains he rose to go back to Dörfli and find lodgings. The grandfather put the box of cakes, the big sausage, and the shawl under his arm; the doctor took Heidi by the hand, and they went down the mountain to goatherd Peter's hut. Here Heidi was to wait until her grandfather came for her, after accompanying his guest down to the village.

"Would you like to go to the pasture tomorrow?" Heidi asked the doctor, for the pasture was the loveliest place she knew.

"To be sure," he replied. "We will go together."

After the men had gone, Heidi went into the grandmother's hut. First, she dragged in the box of cakes; then she had to go out again to bring in the other presents, for her grandfather had laid everything down in front of the door. She brought them as close to the grandmother as possible, so she might touch them and know what they were. She laid the warm gray shawl in the old lady's lap.

"The presents are from Klara and her grandmamma," she explained. "Surely, grandmother, you are pleased with the cakes, aren't you?"

"Yes, indeed, Heidi; what good people they are!" said the astonished grandmother, stroking the gray shawl. "But this is something splendid for the cold winter! I never dreamed I should ever own anything so magnificent."

Heidi was surprised that the grandmother should be more delighted with the gray shawl than with the cakes. Meanwhile Brigitte stood staring at the big sausage on the table. In all her life she had never seen such a giant sausage, and that she was going to have it for her own seemed too good to be true.

"We must ask the uncle what it is meant for," she said timidly.

"It is meant to eat, and nothing else," said Heidi.

At this moment Peter came stumbling in. "The Alm-Uncle is coming just behind me. Heidi must—"

His eyes fell on the table, and the sight of the sausage so overpowered him that he could not say another word.

The Alm-Uncle never went by the hut now without stopping to speak to the grandmother. But today it was late, and Heidi must have her sleep. So he merely called good night through the open door and took Heidi's hand as she ran to meet him. Then the two of them made their way under the twinkling stars back to their peaceful hut.

Chapter 3

CONSOLATION

~~~~~~

EARLY THE next morning the doctor climbed the mountain from Dörfli in company with Peter and his goats. He tried several times to enter into conversation with the goatboy, but he did not succeed in getting more than the briefest answers to his questions. So they traveled in silence up to the Alm hut, where Heidi stood waiting with her two goats.

"Coming, too?" asked Peter, for he said this every morning.

"Of course, if the doctor will come with us," replied Heidi.

Peter looked a little askance at the gentleman.

Then the grandfather came out, bringing the dinner bag in his hand. He greeted the doctor, then went to Peter and hung the bag over his shoulder.

It was heavier than usual, for the uncle had put in a good piece of the dried meat; he thought possibly the doctor might like it up in the pasture. Peter's mouth spread almost from one ear to the other with a grin of satisfaction, for he suspected that there was something unusual inside.

The journey up the mountain began, with Heidi surrounded by the goats. Each one wanted to be near her, until finally she stood still and said:

"Now please run away and don't keep pushing and jostling me. I must go with the doctor a little while now."

She patted Schneehöpli gently on the back, then made her way out of the flock and ran to the side of the doctor. He took her hand, and as they climbed, she told him about the birds and the flowers and the remarkable doings of the goats. Meanwhile Peter had been casting sidewise glances at the doctor. These glances might have terrified him, but fortunately he did not see them.

When they reached the end of their journey, Heidi took her kind friend to the loveliest spot of all, and he dropped down beside her on the sunny ground. The autumn sun shone over the peaks and the distant green valley. From the pastures below came the peaceful sound of herd bells. A gentle breeze softly stirred the last bluebells. The robber-bird flew in wide circles above them, but today he did not scream. With outspread wings he seemed to float through the air and take his ease.

Heidi's eyes sparkled with delight. She looked at her friend to see if he appreciated how lovely everything was.

"Yes, Heidi, it is beautiful here," he said. "But if one has a sad heart, how can one enjoy this beauty?"

"Oh, oh!" exclaimed Heidi quite gayly. "Nobody ever has a sad heart here—only in Frankfurt."

A smile passed over the doctor's face, but quickly vanished. Then he added: "But supposing someone should come and bring his sorrow with him from Frankfurt. Do you know of anything that could help him then?"

"He must tell everything to the dear Lord, if he does not know what to do," said Heidi with perfect assurance.

"Yes, that is a good thought, child," observed the doctor. "But if your sorrow comes from him, what can you say to the dear Lord?"

Heidi had to think what ought to be done in such a case. She was certain that one could obtain help from the dear Lord for every sorrow. She sought a reply from her own experience.

"Then you must wait," she said, "and keep thinking: 'Surely now the dear Lord knows some joy which is to come out of this by and by.' Then all at once you will see quite clearly that the dear Lord had nothing but good in his mind all the time."

"That is a beautiful faith, and you must hold it fast," said the doctor, gazing down into the green sunlit valley. "You see, Heidi, you might sit here with a great shade over your eyes, so that you could not take in the beauty all about. Then indeed would your heart be doubly sad, because everything is so beautiful. Can you understand that?"

Heidi nodded sadly. The doctor's words about a shade over the eyes reminded her of the grandmother who could never see again. After a long silence she said earnestly:

"Yes, indeed, I can understand that. But you must say the grandmother's hymns, and they will give you a little light, perhaps so much light that you will become quite happy. The grandmother said so."

"What hymns, Heidi?" asked the doctor.

"I know only the one about the sun and the beautiful garden, and the verses the grandmother likes from the other long one. I always have to read it three times," replied Heidi.

"Say the verses for me, Heidi," said the doctor.

"Shall I begin where the grandmother says that trust returns to one's heart?"

The doctor nodded. Then Heidi began:

> "*Oh, trust His love to guide thee,*
> *He is a Prince so wise*
> *That what His hands provide thee*
> *Is wondrous in thine eyes.*
> *And He, if He be willing,*
> *May bring the work about*
> *And thus thy hopes fulfilling*
> *Dispel thy fear and doubt.*

It may be for a season
He will no comfort show,
And for some hidden reason
His light will not bestow.
As if no more He heeded
What sorrow was thy share,
Or what relief thou needed
In all thy deep despair.

But if thy sure faith stays thee
When thou are most perplexed,
He will appear and raise thee
What time thou least expect'st.
He will remove the burden
That presses thy heart down,
And thou shalt have the guerdon
And thou shalt wear the crown."

Heidi stopped, for she was not sure that the doctor was still listening. He had put his hand over his eyes and was sitting motionless. She thought perhaps he had fallen asleep. But the doctor was not asleep. He had been carried back to the days of long ago when, as a little boy, he had stood beside his mother's chair. He could almost hear her voice as she sang the hymn that Heidi had just repeated. He sat for a long time, with his face buried in his hands. When he finally rose, he noticed that Heidi was looking at him in amazement. He took the child's hand in his.

"Heidi, your hymn was beautiful," he said, his voice sounding more cheerful. "We will come up here another day, and you shall say it for me again."

While Heidi talked with the doctor, Peter had been growing

more impatient. She had not been up in the pasture for several days. Now that she had come, this old gentleman sat beside her the whole time, and she paid no attention to anyone else.

This greatly annoyed Peter. He took his place on a slope higher up where the unsuspecting doctor could not see him. He doubled up his fist and shook it. After a while, he doubled up both fists. The longer Heidi remained sitting beside the doctor, the more frantically Peter shook his fists.

When the sun stood high in the sky, Peter knew it was time for the midday meal.

"We must have something to eat!" he called.

Heidi rose and was going to get the bag so that the doctor could have his dinner just where he was sitting. But he said he was not hungry; he wanted nothing but a glass of milk to drink and then he would like to climb a little higher on the mountain. Suddenly Heidi discovered that she was not hungry either, and that she cared for only a glass of milk too. Then she would like to take the doctor to the big moss-covered rock, high up, where the spicy herbs grew. She ran to Peter and explained that he must first take a bowl of milk from Schwänli for the doctor and another for herself.

"Who is to have what is in the bag?" asked Peter.

"You may have it, but you must get the milk first and be quick about it," was Heidi's reply.

Peter had never done anything in his life so quickly as he accomplished this task. As soon as Heidi and the doctor had drunk their milk, he opened the bag. When he saw the big piece of meat, his whole body trembled with delight. He put in his hand, then suddenly drew it back, as though he dared not take such a wonderful present. He remembered how he had shaken his fist at the doctor, and this kept him from enjoying the dinner the doctor had given him.

He jumped up and ran back to the place where he had been standing, stretched both hands wide open up in the air, as a sign that his clinched fists had meant nothing. He remained standing there for some time until he felt that his deed was atoned for. Then he took great leaps back to the bag, now that his conscience was clear he could enjoy his nice dinner.

The doctor and Heidi wandered about together for a long while. When he decided that it was time for him to go back, Heidi insisted on walking with him as far as her grandfather's hut. She went hand in hand with her friend, and on the way she had a great deal to show him. She wanted him to see the places where the goats liked best to feed, and where grew the greatest number of yellow wild roses and red centauries and other flowers to be found in the summertime. She knew them all, for her grandfather had taught her their names.

But at last the doctor said he must go. They bade each other good night, and as he went down the mountain, he turned every little while to look back. He saw Heidi standing in the same place, waving her hand to him. Just so his own dear little daughter had waved when he went away from his house.

It was a clear, sunny autumn month. Every morning the doctor came up on the mountain. Often he went off with the Alm-Uncle far up into the craggy mountains, where the old weather-beaten fir trees grew. The great robber-bird must have had his nest near by, for he often whizzed past, whirring and croaking.

The doctor took great pleasure in his companion's society, and was amazed to see how familiar the uncle was with all the plants on his mountain, and how well he knew what they were good for. The old man was equally familiar with the life and habits of the animals up there, both big and small. He had very amusing things to tell the doctor about the ways of the little creatures living in holes in the rocks, in caves, and even in the branches of the lofty fir trees.

The doctor did not know where the time went on these excursions, and often at evening when he shook the uncle's hand at parting, he would say:

"My good friend, I never go away from you without learning something new."

But usually the doctor chose to go with Heidi. They would sit together on the lovely cliff where they had sat the first day, and Heidi repeated her hymns. Peter would sit behind them in his place, but he was now quite peaceable and no longer shook his fists at them.

At last the doctor had to return to Frankfurt. The parting

grieved him, for he loved the mountain like his own home. Heidi had become so used to seeing him every day that it was hard for her to realize his visit was coming to an end. The doctor bade her grandfather farewell, then asked her to walk with him a little way. Hand in hand they started down the mountain.

Finally the doctor stood still. Heidi had come far enough, he said, and must turn back. He laid his hand tenderly on her curly hair.

"I must go, Heidi," he said. "If only I could take you to Frankfurt and keep you with me!"

A shadow passed over Heidi's face as she remembered Frankfurt with its many, many houses and stony streets. She thought of Fräulein Rottenmeier and Tinette, and she answered timidly:

"I would rather have you come back to us again."

"Well, yes, that would be better, so good-by," said the doctor, holding out his hand. When Heidi looked up at him, she saw that the kind eyes had filled with tears. Then he turned away and hurried down the mountain.

Heidi remained standing where he had left her. The sight of his tears had gone straight to her heart. Suddenly she burst into loud weeping and rushed after him.

"Doctor! Doctor!" she called.

He turned around and waited until she reached him. The tears were streaming down her cheeks.

"I will go with you to Frankfurt now, and I will stay with you as long as you like, but I must hurry back to tell my grandfather."

"No, my dear Heidi," he said kindly, "not now. You must stay under the fir trees for you might be sick again if you went with me. But I want to ask you something. If I am ever sick and alone, will you come then and stay with me? Can I think then that someone will care for me and love me?"

"Yes, yes; then I will surely come to you, the very same day.

And I love you almost as well as my grandfather," said Heidi decidedly.

The doctor pressed her hand once more and hurried on his way. But Heidi remained standing in the same spot, waving until he seemed like a mere speck in the distance. When he turned around for the last time to look back at her, he said softly to himself:

"It is good to be on the mountain. Body and soul get well there, and life becomes happy again."

Chapter 4

THE WINTER IN DÖRFLI

AROUND THE ALM hut the snow lay so deep that it looked as if the windows were on a level with the ground. The house door had completely disappeared. If the Alm-Uncle had been up there, he would have had to do what Peter did every day. Each morning the goatherd jumped out of the window, sinking deep in the soft snow which had fallen during the night. He pushed and kicked in every direction until he worked his way out. Then his mother handed him a broom through the window, and with this he shoved the snow before him until he reached the door. There all the snow had to be dug away.

But freezing weather brought many conveniences to Peter. If he was going down to Dörfli, all he had to do was to open the window and crawl out on the smooth, firm surface of the snow field. His mother would push his little sled through the window after him, and Peter had only to seat himself on it and slide wherever he liked. The whole Alm was one great unbroken slope.

The uncle had kept his word. As soon as the first snow had fallen he had shut up the hut and shed and had gone down to Dörfli with Heidi and the goats. Near the church stood a spacious building, which in old times had been a great mansion, although now it was more or less in ruins. A brave warrior had once lived in it; he had gone to the Spanish wars and had never come back. When it was known that he was really dead, a distant relative down in the valley took the house, but it was already tumbling to pieces, and the new owner did not care to build it up again.

Since that time, many years had passed. When the uncle had returned to Dörfli with his son, Tobias, he had rented part of the ruined house and lived in it. Since then it had stood empty most of the time for no one without skill to mend the holes and gaps could stay there. The winter in Dörfli was long and cold. The wind blew in from every side through the rooms, but the uncle knew how to manage. As soon as he had made up his mind to spend the winter in the village, he took the old house again, and often during the autumn came down to mend and repair it as he liked. About the middle of October he brought Heidi down from the mountain to live there.

Entering the house from the rear, one came at once into an open room. The entire wall on one side and half on the other had fallen in. Above this an arched window was still to be seen, but the glass had long been out of it, and thick ivy crept around it and high up on the roof. The window was beautifully arched, for the room had been at one time a chapel. From here one went into a large hall, paved with what once were handsome tiles. The tiles were broken now, and the grass grew between them. The walls were half gone, and great pieces of the roof had given way.

Here the uncle had put up a partition of boards and had covered the floor thickly with hay. In this old hall the goats were to be housed.

Then there were all sorts of passageways, half uncovered, so that the sky could be seen through them. But in the front, where the heavy oaken door still hung firmly on its hinges, there was a spacious room which was still in good condition. The four walls were all standing, and the dark wainscotings showed not a break. In one corner stood a huge stove, reaching almost to the ceiling, and on the white tiles were big blue pictures of old castles, with tall trees all around, and a huntsman passing with his dogs. There

was another picture of a peaceful lake with a fisherman holding his rod far out over the water.

This stove was the first thing Heidi noticed. Around it there was a circular bench, and she sat down to look at the pictures. Soon something new took her attention. In the large space behind the stove, between it and the wall, were four boards. At first Heidi thought she was looking at a bin for apples, but there were no apples in it. She looked again and saw that it had been filled with hay, with a linen sheet on top and a bag for a coverlet. There was Heidi's bed, exactly as it had been in the hut on the Alm.

"Oh, grandfather," she shouted, "here is my bedroom! Oh, how lovely! But where will you sleep?"

"Your bedroom must be near the stove so you won't freeze," said her grandfather. "You may see mine too."

Heidi skipped across the big room after her grandfather, who opened a door on the other side. This led into a little room where he had arranged his bed. Still another door opened into a sort of kitchen, more enormous than any she had ever seen. There were holes and wide cracks in the walls on all sides, where the wind blew in, although so many had been nailed up with boards that it looked as if little cupboards had been made all around the wall.

Heidi was well pleased with her new dwelling place, and she lost no time in exploring every nook and corner. By the time Peter came the next day to see how she was getting along, she felt thoroughly at home and could take him everywhere. She gave him no rest until he had seen all the wonderful things in the old house.

When night came, Heidi slept soundly in her chimney corner. But when she awoke in the morning she missed the sound of the wind roaring through the branches of the fir trees. At first she had to look around her for a long while until she remembered where she was. When she realized that she was not at home on the mountain, she seemed to feel something stifling her and pressing against her heart.

But when she heard her grandfather talking outside with Schwänli and Bärli, she felt as if she were at home after all. The goats bleated loudly and merrily, as if they were calling to her, and she jumped gaily out of bed and hurried to the big goat barn.

On the fourth day Heidi said:

"Today I must really go up to see the grandmother. She can't be alone so long."

But her grandfather did not agree. "Not today, nor tomorrow

either," he said. "The Alm is six feet deep with snow. Peter can hardly get through. A little thing like you, Heidi, would be snowed in and covered up the first thing, and you never could be found again. Wait until it freezes. Then you can easily walk over the crust."

Heidi was disappointed to have to wait, but the days were so full of work that they passed quickly. Every morning and afternoon she went to school and was quick in learning all her lessons. She hardly ever saw Peter in school, for he seldom came. The teacher was a meek man and only now and then said:

"It seems to me Peter is absent again. School would do him good. But there is a great deal of snow on the Alm. Perhaps he can't get through."

But toward evening, when school was out, Peter usually got through and paid a visit to Heidi.

After a few days, the sun came out again and threw its rays over the white earth. But it went down behind the mountains again very early, as if it was not so well pleased to look down as in summer, when everything was green and in bloom. In the evening, the moon shone over the vast snow fields, and the next day the whole mountain glittered like a crystal.

One morning, when Peter jumped out of the window, something happened he had not expected. Instead of coming down into the soft snow, he landed on a surprisingly hard surface, and before he knew it, he had slipped a good piece down the mountain, like an empty sled. Very much surprised he finally succeeded in getting on his feet again. He stamped with all his might on the crust, but he could scarcely break off the least bit of ice. The whole Alm was frozen as hard as a rock.

Peter was glad, for he knew this meant that Heidi could come up on the mountain for a visit. He went back into the hut, drank the milk which his mother put on the table and tucked his piece of bread into his pocket.

"I must go to school," he said.

"Yes, do go and study hard," said his mother encouragingly.

Peter crawled through the window, for now they were shut in again on account of the heaps of ice before the door. He pulled his little sled after him, sat down on it, and shot down the mountain. It went like lightning, and when he came near to Dörfli, he was unable to bring it to a stop. It shot right past the village, down the slope toward Mayenfeld. So he went on until he reached level ground and the sled stopped of itself. Then he got up and looked around. The force of the descent had carried him beyond Mayenfeld.

Since it was now too late for school, he decided he might as well take his time about climbing back up the mountain. This he did, and he reached Dörfli just as Heidi was sitting down to dinner with her grandfather.

"We've got it," said Peter, standing still in the middle of the room.

"Got what, general?" said the uncle.

"The crust," replied Peter.

"Oh! oh! Now I can go up to see the grandmother!" Heidi shouted joyfully. "But why didn't you come to school then? You could slide down well enough."

"Went too far on my sled," replied Peter.

"That is called desertion," said the uncle; "and people who desert are taken by the ears! Do you hear?"

Peter pulled down his cap in alarm.

"Besides, a leader like you are ought to be doubly ashamed of running away," continued the uncle. "What would you think if your goats should run, one this way and another that, and refuse to follow you and do what was good for them? What would you do then?"

"Beat them," replied Peter knowingly.

"And if a boy behaves like an unruly goat and is beaten a little, what would you say to that?"

"Serves him right," was the answer.

"Well, now understand, goatcolonel, if you go past the school on your sled again, come here to me and get what you deserve."

Then Peter understood what the Alm-Uncle meant: that a boy who played truant was like an unruly goat. He looked anxiously into the corner to see whether he could discover what the uncle used at such times for the goats.

"Come to the table now," said the uncle cheerfully. "Then Heidi may go with you. If you bring her back home at evening, you will find your supper here."

This unexpected turn of affairs was highly delightful to Peter. He sat down, and the uncle filled his plate with a big potato and toasted cheese. Heidi ran to the cupboard and brought out the little cloak Klara had given her. As soon as Peter had shoved in his last mouthful she said:

"Now come!"

On the way Heidi had a great deal to tell Peter about Schwänli and Bärli: how neither of them had eaten anything the first day in their new barn, but had hung their heads and not made a sound. She had asked her grandfather why they did so, and he said that they felt just as she had in Frankfurt, for they had never been down from the Alm in all their lives. And Heidi added:

"You just ought to know once what that is, Peter."

The two had almost reached the end of their journey before Peter spoke a word. But before entering the hut, he stood still and said somewhat crossly:

"There! I would rather go to school than take from the uncle what he promised."

"Of course," agreed Heidi, "and I'll help you with your lessons."

Inside the hut, Peter's mother was sitting alone with her mending. The grandmother was not well and was spending the day in bed. When Heidi heard this, she ran into the old lady's room and found her wrapped up in the gray shawl in her narrow bed with the thin covering.

"God be praised and thanked!" said the grandmother. All autumn she had had a secret anxiety in her heart. Peter had reported how a strange gentleman from Frankfurt had been there, and the grandmother was afraid that he might take Heidi away again.

"Are you very ill, grandmother?" asked Heidi.

"No, no," said the old lady soothingly, while she stroked the child's face affectionately. "The cold weather has got into my limbs a little."

"Will you be well, as soon as it is warm again?" asked Heidi eagerly.

"Yes, God willing; even before that, so that I can get to my spinning wheel. I even thought today that I would try it. Tomorrow it will surely be going again," said the grandmother, for she had noticed that the child was alarmed.

Her words soothed Heidi, who had never found the grandmother sick in bed before. She looked at her in surprise.

"In Frankfurt," she said, "people put on their shawls when they go outdoors. Do you think you ought to wear yours in bed?"

"I wrap the shawl around me so I won't freeze," said the grandmother. "I am so glad to have it for the bed covering is rather thin."

"But, grandmother," Heidi began again, "your head goes downhill, where it ought to go up. A bed ought not to be like that."

"I know it, child." The grandmother tried to find a better place for the pillow that lay like a thin board under her head. "You see the pillow was never thick, and now I have slept so many years on it that I have made it rather flat."

"Oh, if only I had asked Klara when I was in Frankfurt to let me take my bed home with me!" exclaimed Heidi. "It had three big, thick pillows, one on top of another. Sometimes I would slip down off them to where the bed was flat. Could you sleep on three pillows, grandmother?"

"Yes, indeed. They would keep me warm, and I could breathe more easily if I could lie with my head high," said the grandmother, lifting her head rather wearily, as if to find a higher place for it. "But we won't talk about that. I have to thank the dear Lord for so much that other sick old people do not have: the nice rolls you give me and this warm shawl, and your coming to see me, Heidi. Will you read something to me again today?"

Heidi fixed the pillows so the grandmother could sit straighter.

Then she ran out and brought back the old hymn book. She read one beautiful song after another, while the grandmother lay with folded hands and listened with a happy smile.

Suddenly Heidi stopped.

"Grandmother, you look so much better. Are you well again already?"

"I'm feeling much better. What you have read to me has done me good. Finish it, will you?"

The child read the hymn to the end, and when she came to the last words,

> *"When mine eyes grow dimmer, sadder,*
> *Pour the light into my heart,*
> *That I may pass over gladder*
> *Than men to their homes depart,"*

the grandmother repeated them over and over. There was such an expression of joy on her face that Heidi was reminded of her own journey home.

"Grandmother," she said, "I know how it feels to be on the way home. But it is growing dark now and I must go back. I am so glad that you are happy again."

The grandmother took the child's hand in hers and held it fast. "Yes, I am happy again. You see, nobody who has not been an invalid knows what it is to have to lie for days and days all alone, and not be able to see—not see even a single sunbeam. Such gloomy thoughts come to me that I feel I cannot bear it. But when I hear the words you have just read, a light seems to shine in my heart."

Outside the moon shone so brightly that it seemed as if daylight had come back. Heidi sat down behind Peter on his sled, and away they shot, like two birds rushing through the air.

Later, lying in her soft, deep bed of hay, she was thinking of the grandmother. Perhaps, if she could hear the words of the hymns every day, she would be well again. But a week, perhaps two, must pass before Heidi could go back and read to her.

Then all at once Heidi had a wonderful idea, and she could hardly wait until morning to carry out her plan.

Chapter 5

PETER LEARNS TO READ

~~~~~~

PETER ARRIVED at school on time the next morning, and in the afternoon he went to the Alm-Uncle's to see Heidi.

"I know something, Peter," she said eagerly.

"Say it," he replied.

"You must learn to read," she answered.

"Can't learn," said Peter.

"Nobody believes such a thing as that, and I don't either," said Heidi decidedly. "The grandmamma in Frankfurt knew it wasn't true, and she told me that I ought not to believe it either." Peter was dumfounded at this news.

"I will teach you to read; I know how very well," Heidi continued. "You must learn right away; then you can read one or two hymns every day to your grandmother."

"Don't want to," grumbled Peter.

This obstinacy made Heidi angry. With flashing eyes she placed herself in front of the boy and said threateningly:

"Do you know what will happen if you never learn anything? Your mother has already said that you should go to Frankfurt and learn something. And I know where the boys go to school there. Klara showed me the frightfully big house when we were out driving. Instead of having one good, kind teacher, the way we have here, they have whole rows of teachers. I saw them going into the house, dressed in black as though they were going to church. They had high black hats on their heads—"

Heidi paused to measure the size of the hats from the floor up, and Peter shivered.

"And if you made mistakes, they would laugh at you," she said.

"I'll learn to read," said Peter quickly, and Heidi was pacified.

Klara had sent Heidi an ABC book in rhyme, and she had decided that this would be a good thing to use in teaching Peter. She drew him over to the table, sat down beside him and opened the book. She made him spell the first sentence over and over again.

"You don't know it yet," she said finally. "I will read it to you, until you get it into your head. Now listen:

> *"If A, B, C, you do not know,*
> *Before the school board you will go."*

"I will not go," said Peter angrily.

"Where?" asked Heidi.

"Before the school board," said Peter.

"You won't have to if you learn these letters," said Heidi.

So Peter began again and repeated the letters over and over, until Heidi said, "Now you know all three."

Then she picked up the book and began to read clearly.

> *"D, E, F, G must smoothly fly,*
> *Or else misfortune will be nigh.*
>
> *If H, I, J, K, are forgot,*
> *Misfortune is upon the spot.*
>
> *Whoe'er on L, M, still will stumble*
> *Must pay a fine and then feel humble.*
>
> *There's something bad, and if you knew,*
> *You'd quickly learn N, O, P, Q.*

If still on R, S, T, you halt,
The harm that comes will be your fault."

Here Heidi stopped; Peter was staring at her in terror. Heidi's tender heart was touched.

"Don't be frightened," she said. "Just come to me every afternoon, and if you learn as well as you have today, you will know all the letters after a while. Then nothing will happen to you. But you must come every day, and not do the way you go to school. If it snows, it won't do you any harm."

Peter followed Heidi's orders strictly, and every afternoon studied the other letters eagerly and learned the rhymes by heart.

The grandfather often sat in the room and listened to the exercise while he smoked his pipe. Sometimes the corners of his mouth twitched as if he could hardly keep from laughing.

After the great struggle, Peter was usually invited to stay for supper, and he felt rewarded for the anguish the day's lesson had caused him. As the winter days passed, he really made progress, but sometimes he grew discouraged. One afternoon, when they had reached the letter, U, Heidi read the couplet:

"If ever you mix U and V,
You'll go where you'll not like to be."

"Yes, see if I will!" Peter growled.

But he learned the letters thoroughly as though afraid someone might take him secretly by the throat and carry him where he would not care to go.

On the following afternoon Heidi read:

"If now you fail to know the W,
There hangs a stick and it will trouble you."

"There isn't any," said Peter scornfully.

"Yes, there is; don't you know what grandfather has in the chest?" asked Heidi. "A stick as big around as my arm, and when he takes it out he can say:

" 'Behold the stick, and it will trouble you.' "

Peter knew the big hazel stick. He bent over the W at once and tried to learn it.

The next day Heidi read:

"If you the letter X forget,
For you no supper will be set."

Peter looked inquiringly toward the cupboard and said snappishly, "I have never said I would forget X."

"That is right, if you don't forget it," Heidi answered. "Now if you'll learn one more letter, there will only be one left for you to learn tomorrow."

And Heidi read:

"*If you on Y today delay,*
With scorn and shame you'll go away."

Peter thought of all the masters in Frankfurt with their tall, black hats and with scorn and ridicule on their faces. He immediately attacked the letter Y, and soon knew it so well that he could close his eyes and still see how it looked.

On the next day, Peter was feeling rather proud when he came to Heidi, for there was only one letter left for him to study. When Heidi read the verse:

"*Who hesitates upon the Z,*
With the Hottentots shall be."

he said sneeringly:

"Yes, when nobody knows where they are!"

"Indeed, Peter, my grandfather knows," said Heidi. "Just wait and I will ask him; he is over at the pastor's house." She jumped up and started toward the door.

"Wait!" cried Peter in alarm. In his imagination he saw the Alm-Uncle coming in with the pastor, and the two seizing him at once and sending him off to the Hottentots, for he really did not know the name of Z. His troubled cry made Heidi stand still.

"What is the matter with you?" she asked in surprise.

"Nothing! Come back! I will learn it," stammered Peter. So

Heidi came back and made him repeat the letter Z so many times that he would remember it forever. Then she went on to syllables, and Peter learned so much that afternoon that he made a great advance.

The crust had become soft again, and every day there was a fresh fall of snow. For three long weeks Heidi could not go up to see the grandmother. This made her all the more eager to teach Peter to read the hymns.

One evening Peter came home from Heidi's, and ran into the room in great excitement.

"I can do it," he shouted.

"What can you do, Peterli?" asked his mother.

"I can read," he answered.

"Is it possible! Did you hear, grandmother?" exclaimed Brigitte.

"Now I must read a hymn, for Heidi said so," Peter went on. He took the book down from the shelf, opened it and began to read.

"Who could have thought it?" said his mother.

The grandmother was delighted; it had been so long since she had heard the good words.

The next day Peter's class had a reading lesson. When Peter's turn came the teacher said:

"Peter, must I pass by you as usual, or will you try once more— I will not say read. Will you try to stammer through a line?"

Peter read three lines, one after another without stopping. The teacher looked at him in astonishment.

"Why, you could never even grasp the alphabet, though I tried hard enough to teach you," he said at last. "Now you can read quite easily and clearly. Who was able to work such a miracle, Peter?"

"Heidi," was the reply.

The teacher looked at Heidi in surprise.

"I have noticed other changes in you, Peter," he went on. "You used to be absent from school a whole week—yes, several weeks together. But lately you have not stayed away a day. Who can have caused such a change for the better in you?"

"The uncle," was the reply.

With increasing astonishment the teacher looked from Peter to Heidi, and from her back again to Peter.

"We will try it once more," he said cautiously, and Peter had to prove his knowledge with three more lines. It was a fact, he had learned to read.

As soon as school was over, the teacher hastened to the pastor's house to tell him what had happened, and what a good influence the uncle and Heidi were having in the parish.

Every evening Peter read a hymn at home. He was obeying Heidi, but he never tried to read a second one. Nor did the grandmother ask him to.

"We can't be too pleased that Peterli has learned to read so well," said his mother. "Now there's no knowing what he may become."

"Yes, it is a good thing for him that he has learned something," said the grandmother. "But I wish it was spring, so Heidi could come. When she reads the hymns, they seem different. Peter often leaves something out, and it is hard for me to follow the thought."

This was true, because when Peter came to a hard word he preferred to leave it out. He thought it would be all the same to the grandmother if there were only three or four words in a line. So it happened that there were hardly any nouns left in the hymns that Peter read.

Chapter 6

DISTANT FRIENDS ARE HEARD FROM

~~~~~~

MAY HAD come. From every height the overflowing brooks were rushing down into the valley. Warm, bright sunshine lay on the mountain. It had grown green again; the last traces of snow had melted away, and the first little flowers were peeping up out of the fresh grass. The spring wind blew through the fir trees and shook off the old, dark needles, so that the young, bright green ones could come out and dress the trees in splendor. High above, the old robber-bird was swinging his wings in the blue air, and around the Alm hut the golden sunshine lay warm on the ground.

Heidi was on the mountain again. She ran here and there and could not tell which spot was the loveliest. She liked to listen to the wind as it blew down from the cliffs above, coming nearer and growing mightier, and then leaping into the fir trees, bending and shaking them until it seemed as if it were shouting with delight. Heidi shouted, too, while she was blown hither and thither like a little leaf. Then she would run back to the sunny spot in front of the house, sit down on the ground and peep into the short grass to see how many flower-cups were open.

From the workshop behind the house, every now and then, came the sound of busy hammering and sawing. One day when Heidi ran in to see what her grandfather was doing, he had just finished a fine new stool and was working on another.

"Oh, I know what that is for," cried Heidi. "It is for the grandmamma when she comes from Frankfurt. The stool you are making now is for Klara. But we'll have to have one more. Do you think—" she hesitated—"that Fräulein Rottenmeier will come with them?"

"I can't say now," said her grandfather, "but it will be safer to have one ready, so that we can invite her to sit down if she comes."

Heidi looked critically at the little wooden stool and wondered how it would suit Fräulein Rottenmeier. "Grandfather, I don't believe she would sit on it," she said doubtfully.

"Then we will invite her to use the sofa with the beautiful green grass covering," replied the grandfather quietly.

Suddenly there came from above a whistling and calling and the sound of a rod swinging through the air. Heidi ran out and in a twinkling was surrounded by the leaping goats. They must have been glad to be up on the mountain again, for they jumped higher and bleated more merrily than they had ever done before. But Heidi had no time to play with them today, for Peter handed her a letter.

"Did you find a letter for me up in the pasture?" she asked in astonishment.

"No," was the answer.

This was true. The postmaster in Dörfli had given the letter to Peter the evening before, and he had put it in the empty bag. That morning he had put his bread and cheese in on top of it, and had forgotten all about it until he ate his lunch.

Heidi read the address and ran back to her grandfather in the shop. "Here's a letter from Frankfurt. From Klara. Will you hear it now, Grandfather?"

He was very ready to hear it. So was Peter, who followed Heidi into the shop and leaned with his back against the doorpost to have a firm support while he listened.

Heidi opened the letter and began to read:

"DEAR HEIDI: Everything is packed, and in two or three days we shall start on our journey. The doctor comes every day and calls out at the door: 'Away! Away! To the mountains!' He is impatient for us to be off. You know how much he liked it on the Alm! He has come to see us almost every day all winter, and he told me all about the days he spent with you and your grandfather, about the mountains and the flowers, and the stillness so high above all the villages, and about the fine fresh air. He often said: 'Everybody ought to get well up there.' He is so different from what he had been for a long time, and looks quite young and happy again.

"Oh, how glad I shall be to see you on the mountain, and learn to know Peter and the goats! But first I have to take the cure in Ragatz for about six weeks; the doctor has ordered it. Afterwards we shall stay in Dörfli, and I shall be carried up on the mountain in my chair, in fine weather, to spend the day with you.

"Grandmamma is coming, too. But think of it, Fräulein Rottenmeier will not come with us. Almost every day grandmamma says to her:

" 'How is it about the journey to Switzerland, worthy Rottenmeier? If you would like to come with us, you can do so.'

"But she always thanks grandmamma very politely and says she wouldn't be so presuming. But I know what she is thinking about. Sebastian gave a frightful description of the mountains when he came back from going with you—what terrible overhanging crags there were, and what danger there was everywhere of falling down into the chasms and ravines. Fräulein Rottenmeier shuddered, and since then has not been enthusiastic about traveling in Switzerland, as she was before. Tinette too has become frightened and will not come with us. So we are coming alone, grandmamma and I. I can hardly wait.

"Good-by, dear Heidi. Grandmamma sends you a thousand greetings.

"Your true friend,

"KLARA."

When Peter heard these words, he ran out of the shed. He struck out right and left so recklessly with his rod that the terrified goats took to flight and ran down the mountain. He rushed after them, beating the air with his rod, as if he had to vent his spite on some invisible enemy. This enemy was the prospect of guests coming from Frankfurt.

Heidi was so full of happiness that she decided to visit the grandmother the next day and tell her all about it. She found the old lady sitting once more in the corner spinning. She seemed troubled, for Peter had come home in great anger the night before. From his mumblings she had understood that a crowd of people from Frankfurt was coming up to the Alm hut. What would happen afterwards he did not know. The grandmother had been so worried that she could not sleep.

Heidi sat down on the little footstool near the spinning wheel and began to tell her good news. Suddenly she stopped in the middle of a sentence.

"What is the matter, grandmother? Don't you like all this a single bit?"

"Yes, Heidi, I am glad for you, because it will give you so much pleasure."

"But, grandmother, I can see that it troubles you. Do you think Fräulein Rottenmeier will come with them?" asked Heidi, feeling somewhat anxious herself.

"No, no! It is nothing!" said the grandmother soothingly. "Let me take your hand, Heidi, so I can feel you are still here. It will be a good thing for you, even if I don't live to see that day."

"I don't care for what is best for me, if you are not going to live to see it, grandmother," said Heidi, so decidedly.

The grandmother was silent. She took it for granted that the people from Frankfurt would want to take Heidi home with them, now that she was well again. This was a great grief to the grandmother. But she felt that she ought not to say anything about it, because Heidi would feel so sorry for her that she might object to going. And that must not happen.

"I know something," she said, "that will make me feel better and bring me good thoughts again. Read me the hymn that begins, 'God will bring.'"

Heidi had become so familiar with the old hymn book that she found the place at once and read in a clear voice:

"God will bring
Everything
Into order as is wholesome for thy soul.
Thou shalt be
Safe at sea
Though the foaming billows wildly round thee roll."

"Yes, that is exactly what I want to hear," said the grandmother, relieved, and the expression of distress disappeared. When evening came and Heidi was climbing up the mountain again, one little star after another came out and twinkled down at her. She had to stand still every few minutes and look up at them. When she reached the hut, her grandfather was standing out in front, also gazing at the stars, for they had not shone so beautifully for a long time.

One morning more than a month later Heidi was playing in front of the hut, when suddenly she called:

"Grandfather! Grandfather! Come here! See! See!"

The Alm-Uncle rushed outdoors to find the child almost beside herself with excitement. A strange procession was winding up the Alm. First came two men with a sedan chair in which sat a young girl wrapped in shawls. Then came a stately lady riding a horse and talking with the guide walking at her side. Another guide was pushing an empty wheel chair, and last of all came a porter, with so many wraps and shawls and furs piled up in the basket on his back that they reached high above his head.

"There they are! There they are!" squealed Heidi.

Klara and her grandmamma really were coming. They came nearer and nearer and at last they were there. The porter put the chair down on the ground. Heidi ran to it and the two children greeted each other with delight. The grandmamma dismounted from the horse and embraced Heidi with great tenderness. Then she turned to the Alm-Uncle, who had come forward to welcome her. There was no formality in their greeting; they felt as though they had known each other for a long time.

"My dear uncle," said the grandmamma, "what a wonderful location you have! A king might envy you, it is so glorious all about! What do you say, Klärchen, my child!"

Klara was looking around her, perfectly enchanted. "How beautiful it is here!" she exclaimed again and again. "I never imagined anything like it. Oh, I wish I could stay!"

Meanwhile the uncle had pushed along the wheel chair, taken

some shawls out of the basket, and arranged them in it. Then
he stepped up to the sedan chair.

"If we put the little daughter in her accustomed chair now,
it would be better for her; the traveling chair is a little hard,"
he said. Without waiting for anyone to assist him, he lifted
Klara gently in his strong arms and placed her in the wheel chair.
He tucked a cushion under her feet and wrapped a shawl
around her knees as skilfully as though he had devoted his whole
life to caring for invalids. The grandmamma looked at him in
astonishment.

"My dear uncle," she exclaimed, "if I knew where you learned
to care for the sick, I would send all the nurses I know there to
take lessons. How is it possible?"

The uncle smiled a little sadly. "It comes more from experience
than from study," he replied, remembering the suffering face of
a man who used to sit wrapped up in a chair just like this. It was
his captain, whom he had found lying on the ground after a
fierce battle in Sicily, and had carried off the field. From that
time, the captain had allowed no other nurse around him until
his sufferings came to an end.

The sky was spread like a canopy, deep blue and cloudless,
above the hut and the fir trees and the lofty cliffs. Klara was
fascinated.

"Oh, Heidi, if I could only walk around with you and see
everything!" she said longingly.

Heidi made a great effort and succeeded in rolling the chair
over the smooth, grassy ground under the fir trees. Here she
paused. Klara had never seen anything like the tall old fir trees
with their wide-spreading branches growing down to the ground.
For many years those trees had stood there, looking down into
the valley where men came and went; but the trees had remained.

Then Heidi pushed the wheel chair in front of the goatshed

and opened the little door so Klara could look inside. There was really not much to see, for the goats were not at home. Klara called back regretfully:

"Grandmamma, if I could just wait for Schwänli and Bärli and all the other goats, and Peter! I can never see them if we always have to leave early."

"Dear child, we will enjoy all the beautiful things that are here, and not think about those that are wanting," was the grandmamma's advice.

"Oh, the flowers!" exclaimed Klara. "Whole bushes of fine red flowers, and all the nodding bluebells! If I could only go and get some!"

Heidi ran off and brought back a big bunch of flowers, which she laid in Klara's lap. "But this is nothing," she said. "If you could come up to the pasture with us, then you would really see something. There are ever so many more bluebells than here, and there are so many yellow wild roses that the ground looks like gold. If you once sit down there, you never want to get up, because it is so lovely."

Klara's gentle blue eyes shone with enthusiasm. "Oh, Heidi, if I could only climb around everywhere on the mountain with you!"

"I will push you," said Heidi soothingly. "I know I could do it."

Meanwhile the grandfather had not been idle. The table and chairs were standing by the bench in front of the hut, and everything was ready for the midday meal. The good dinner was steaming in the kettle and roasting on the big fork over the fire inside the hut. It was not long before the grandfather had everything on the table and the whole company sat down.

The grandmamma was enchanted with this dining room from which one could see far down into the valley. A mild breeze fanned the faces of the guests and rustled pleasantly in the fir

trees as if it had been ordered to furnish music for the feast.

"Nothing like this has ever happened to me. It is really glorious!" exclaimed the grandmamma again and again. "But what do I see? I believe you are taking a second piece of toasted cheese, Klärchen!"

Sure enough, a second golden piece of cheese lay on Klara's slice of bread.

"Oh, it tasted so good, grandmamma—better than anything on the table at Ragatz," said Klara.

"Eat away!" said the Alm-Uncle, well pleased. "It is our mountain air which succeeds when the cook fails."

The time passed quickly, for the grandmamma and the Alm-

Uncle had taken a great liking to each other, and the conversation became more and more lively. Finally the grandmamma looked toward the west, and exclaimed:

"We must soon be getting ready, Klärchen. The sun is already going down. The people will be back with the horse and the chair."

An expression of sadness came over Klara's happy face. "Oh, grandmamma," she begged, "just one hour more, or two! We haven't seen the hut yet—or Heidi's bed."

"That is not possible," said the grandmamma. But she, too, wanted to see the hut. So they rose at once from the table, and the uncle directed the chair toward the door. Here it would go no farther; the chair was much too wide for the opening. So the uncle picked Klara up and carried her inside.

The grandmamma walked back and forth, much interested in the Alm-Uncle's well-ordered domestic arrangements. She even climbed the little ladder leading to the hayloft.

"How sweet it smells!" she exclaimed. "It must be a very healthful sleeping room."

The grandfather followed with Klara in his arms, and Heidi climbed up after him. They all stood around Heidi's beautifully-made hay bed. The grandmamma looked at it quite critically, every now and then drawing in deep breaths of the spicy fragrance of the new hay.

"What a jolly place, Heidi!" said Klara. "From your bed you can see into the sky, and you can hear the fir trees roar outside. I have never seen such a jolly, pleasant sleeping room before!"

"I have an idea," said the uncle, "that is if the grandmamma is not opposed to the plan. I believe if we could keep the little daughter up here for a while she would gain strength. I would take care of her myself. You have brought so many shawls and wraps that we could arrange a comfortable, soft bed for her."

Klara and Heidi shouted with joy, and the grandmamma's face lighted up.

"My dear uncle," she exclaimed, "how did you know what I was thinking? I was saying to myself, 'Wouldn't it be wonderful for the child to stay up here? But the nursing! The inconvenience to the host!' Yet you speak of it as if it were nothing at all. I thank you with all my heart."

The uncle carried Klara back to her chair in front of the hut, and Heidi followed. Then he piled all the shawls and fur robes in his arms and climbed back into the hayloft. While the grandmamma looked on, he spread the shawls, one after another, over the hay. There were so many that the bed finally looked like a little fortress.

"Now let a single wisp of hay stick through if it can," said the grandmamma; but the soft wall was so impenetrable that nothing really could stick through. Then she climbed down the ladder, quite satisfied, and went out to the children. They were sitting close together, planning what they would do while Klara stayed on the mountain. But how long would that be? When they asked the grandmamma, she said that the grandfather would know best about that. So the question was laid before him. He answered that in about four weeks they should be able to tell whether the mountain air was helping Klara or not. Then the children shouted, for the prospect of being together so long surpassed all their expectations.

The porters with the chair and the guide with the horse were seen coming up the mountain. When the grandmamma was preparing to mount her horse, Klara exclaimed cheerfully:

"Oh, grandmamma, we won't say farewell, for you will come back every little while to visit us. That will be wonderful, won't it, Heidi?"

Heidi, who had had one pleasure after another that day, could only express her delight by jumping high into the air.

The grandmamma mounted the steady beast, and the uncle took the bridle and led the horse safely down the steep mountain. She had decided that it might be lonely staying in Dörfli without Klara. So she planned to return to Ragatz and take the journey up the mountain ocassionally from there.

Before the uncle returned, Peter came along with his goats. When they saw Heidi sitting by Klara's chair, they all rushed toward her; and in a moment, the two girls were in the midst of the flock. Some one goat was always crowding and pushing to see over another. Each one was called in turn and presented by Heidi to her guest.

In a very short time Klara had made the long-wished-for acquaintance of Schneehöpli, the jolly Distelfinck, the grandfather's clean goats, and all the rest.

Peter looked on, scowling. Later, when he drove the goats on down the mountain, both girls called out pleasantly, "Good night, Peter," but he made no reply. Instead he raised his rod angrily in the air and ran after his frightened flock.

Now came an end to all the lovely things Klara had seen that day on the mountain. When she and Heidi lay on their soft beds in the hayloft, she looked through the round, open window at the twinkling stars.

"Oh, Heidi," she exclaimed, "look! It is just as if we were riding in the sky in a high carriage!"

"Yes, and do you know why the stars are so full of joy, and wink at us so with their eyes?" asked Heidi.

"No; why?" asked Klara.

"They see up in heaven how well the dear Lord directs everything for people, so that we need not worry, because everything will happen for the best. That pleases the stars, and so they wink. But we must not forget our prayers, Klara. We must ask the dear Lord to think of us when he is directing everything so well. Then we shall always be safe and need never be afraid of anything."

So the children sat up in bed and said their evening prayers. Then Heidi laid her head on her round arm and was asleep in a moment. But Klara stayed awake for a long time, for she had never seen anything so wonderful in her life as this sleeping room in the starlight.

For that matter she had hardly ever seen the stars. She had never gone outside the house at night, and the thick curtains at home had always been drawn long before the stars came out. Now whenever she closed her eyes, she had to open them again, to make sure that the stars were still shining. When finally she dropped off to sleep, she could still see them in her dreams.

Chapter 7

ON THE MOUNTAIN

~~~~~~

THE SUN was just coming up behind the crags and casting its golden beams over the hut and down across the valley. Brighter and brighter grew the clouds until the sun came out in all its glory, and rocks and woods and hilltops were bathed in golden light.

Klara had just awakened, and was gazing in amazement at the sunbeams, which danced on her bed. She did not know where she was until she looked at Heidi sleeping beside her. Then the Alm-Uncle, who had climbed quietly up the ladder, asked in a friendly voice:

"Did you sleep well? Are you tired?"

Klara assured him that she was not tired and that, once she had gone to sleep, she had not waked up all night.

This pleased the grandfather, and he set to work to care for her as skilfully as if it had always been his profession to take care of sick children and make them comfortable.

By the time Heidi opened her eyes, her grandfather had helped Klara dress and was carrying her down the ladder. Heidi dressed quickly and scurried down the ladder after them and ran out the door. She stopped in surprise when she saw what the Alm-Uncle had done. The door of the hut was too small to allow Klara's rolling chair to be brought inside under cover. But behind the shop he had loosened two boards, thus forming a large opening. After the chair was pushed inside, the planks were put back in place although they were not fastened.

Heidi came along just as her grandfather was lifting Klara into her chair. Then he took away the boards and wheeled her out of the shop into the sunshine. He left the chair standing in a safe place while he went into the goat-shed, and Heidi ran to Klara's side.

"Oh, Heidi, if only I could stay up here with you!" Klara drew in deep breaths and leaned back in her chair with a feeling of health such as she had never known before. Never in her life had she breathed the fresh morning air outdoors under the open sky. The sunshine felt pleasant and warm on her hands, and she had never imagined it could be like this on the mountain. She turned, first one way and then another, in her chair, to look up into the blue sky and then into the beautiful valley at her feet.

"Now you see it is just as I told you," said Heidi, much pleased. "Here at my grandfather's on the Alm is the loveliest spot in the whole world."

Just then the grandfather came out of the shed carrying two bowls of foaming, snow-white milk. He handed one to Klara and the other to Heidi.

"This will do the little daughter good," he told Klara. "It is milk from Schwänli and will make you strong."

Klara had never tasted goat's milk, so she had to smell of it a little first, to see what it was like. When she saw how eagerly Heidi drank her milk without stopping, she also began to drink. The milk tasted sweet and nourishing, as though there were sugar and cinnamon in it, and she did not put her bowl down until it was empty.

"Tomorrow you will have two bowls," said the grandfather, well satisfied when he saw how Klara had followed Heidi's example.

When Peter appeared with his flock, the Uncle took him aside. "Now listen! From today on let Schwänli do as she likes. She knows where the best feed is. If you have to climb a little, it won't do any harm; go wherever she wishes. In this respect she has more sense than you, and she must have the very best feed, so that she will give the best possible milk. Why are you looking over there as if you would like to swallow somebody? Now, go on, and remember what I have told you!"

Peter was accustomed to follow the uncle's orders. He immediately started off, but he kept turning his head and rolling his eyes.

"You must come too," he called to Heidi. "You must come too if I have to go after Schwänli."

"I can't," Heidi called back. "I can't come with you for a long, long time, as long as Klara is with us. But grandfather has promised that some day we may go up together."

With these words Heidi turned back to Klara. Then Peter shook both fists so threateningly toward the wheel chair that the goats sprang to one side. He sprang after them and, without stopping, ran on up the mountain until he was out of sight, for he was afraid the uncle might have seen him.

Klara and Heidi had planned so much for that day that they did not know where to begin. Heidi suggested that first they write to the grandmamma.

"Must we go into the house to write?" asked Klara. It was so pleasant outdoors that she did not want to go in.

Heidi knew how to manage. She ran into the hut and came back laden with all her school materials and a three-legged stool. She laid her reader and writing book in Klara's lap, so that she could write on them. Then she seated herself on the little stool by the bench, and both girls began a letter. But after every sentence, Klara had to lay her pencil down and look around. Everything was too lovely! A soft wind fanned her face and whispered in the fir trees. Many little insects hummed in the clear air, and a great stillness lay over the sunny landscape. Lofty peaks looked down

on them, and the wide valley below lay wrapped in peace. Only now and then the merry shouts of some shepherd boy sounded through the air, and the echo gave back the tones softly from the crags.

At noon, the grandfather brought out more steaming bowls of milk, for he said the little daughter must stay outdoors as long as there was a ray of light in the sky. When they had finished their milk, Heidi rolled Klara in her chair out under the fir trees. Here they spent the afternoon, telling what had happened to each of them since Heidi left Frankfurt.

Thus the day passed, and before the girls hardly realized it, evening had come. The army of goats came rushing down the mountain, their leader behind them. His brow was wrinkled and there was an angry light in his eyes.

"Good night, Peter!" Heidi called, when she saw that he had no idea of stopping.

"Good night, Peter!" called Klara pleasantly.

He made no reply, except for an angry snort, as he drove the goats on down the mountain.

When Klara saw the grandfather lead Schwänli into the stall to be milked, she could hardly wait.

"It is very strange, Heidi," she said in surprise. "As long as I can remember, I have eaten only because I had to. Everything I took tasted like cod-liver oil, and I have thought a thousand times: 'If only I never had to eat!' But now I can hardly wait until your grandfather comes with the milk."

"Yes, I know how that is," replied Heidi, remembering the day in Frankfurt when everything had stuck in her throat and would not go down.

When the grandfather came back with the little bowls, Klara drank the rich, spicy milk so eagerly that she finished before Heidi.

"May I have a little more?" she asked, holding out her bowl to the grandfather.

He nodded and, taking Heidi's bowl also, went back into the hut. When he returned, each bowl had a thick cover unlike any cover Klara had ever seen. He had taken two slices of bread and spread them thick with sweet yellow butter. Both girls took deep bites of the appetizing slices and the grandfather was pleased.

That night when Klara went to bed, she followed Heidi's example. Her eyes closed at once, and she slept more soundly than she had ever slept before.

The next day and the next passed in the same delightful way. Then came a great surprise for the children. Two strong porters came climbing up the mountain, each carrying on his back a high bed both covered exactly alike with a white brand-new coverlet. The men also brought a letter from the grandmamma. She wrote that these beds were for Klara and Heidi, that the hay beds were to be taken away, and that from this time on Heidi must sleep in a regular bed, furthermore in the winter one of them must be sent down to Dörfli, but the other was to remain in the hut on the Alm, so that Klara would always find it if she came back. The grandmamma praised the children for their long letters and urged them to continue writing every day.

The grandfather went into the hut, threw the contents of Heidi's bed on the big heap of hay, and laid away the covers. Then he came back to help the men carry the two beds up into the loft. He pushed them close together so that the view through the window might be the same from both pillows.

As time went by, Klara became more and more charmed with her new life. She could not say enough about the grandfather's kindness and thoughtful care, and how amusing Heidi was— much more so than in Frankfurt. Every morning her first thought when she awoke was:

"Oh, praise the Lord; I am still on the Alm!"

The grandfather must have felt a remarkable interest in his little charge, for not a day passed when he did not think of something new to strengthen her. Every afternoon he took a walk up among the rocks climbing higher and higher, and every time he brought back a little bundle which scented the air for a long distance and attracted the goats at evening. They all began to bleat and leap and try to push into the shed where the plants lay, for they knew the odor well. But the uncle had made the door fast, because he had not climbed high up on the rocks after the rare plants so the whole crowd of goats might get a good meal without any trouble. The herbs were intended for Schwänli so she might give still richer milk. It was plain to see how this extraordinary care affected her, for she tossed her head in the air more and more vigorously, and her eyes flashed fire.

It was now the third week since Klara had come. For several days, when the grandfather had brought her down in the morning to place her in her chair, he had said:

"Will the little daughter try just once to stand on the ground? Just for a moment?"

Klara had tried to do as he wished. But she had always said, "Oh, it hurts me so," and had clung to him. But each day he had let her try a little longer.

Such a beautiful summer had not been seen on the Alm for many years. Every day the sun shone in a cloudless sky. At evening it threw its purple and rosy light over the rocky peaks and across the snow fields and then disappeared in a blazing sea of gold. According to Heidi the sunset could be seen properly only in the pasture. She told Klara about it again and again. She also talked of the place up on the slope where there were thousands of golden wild roses and so many bluebells that the grass looked blue. Sitting under the fir trees, Heidi had just been telling again about the flowers and the sunset and the fiery rocks. Such a longing seized her to go up there again that she suddenly jumped up and ran to her grandfather, who was sitting in his shop carving.

"Oh, grandfather," she cried. "Will you come with us up to the pasture tomorrow? It is so lovely up there now!"

"I will agree to it," said the grandfather, "but the little daughter must also do me a favor. She must try again, very hard, this evening to stand."

Heidi ran back to Klara with the wonderful news. Klara promised to try to stand as often as the grandfather wished, for she was delighted at the prospect of a trip to the beautiful goat pasture. Heidi was so happy that she called out to Peter as soon as she saw him coming down that evening:

"Peter! Peter! We are coming with you tomorrow to stay all day."

In reply Peter growled like an angry bear. He struck out furiously at the innocent Distelfinck, trotting along beside him. But the alert Distelfinck had noticed the movement at the right time. He made a leap high over Schneehöpli and the blow whizzed in the air.

Klara and Heidi went up to their two beautiful beds so full of their plans for the next day that they decided to stay awake all night to talk about them. But scarcely had they touched their soft pillows when they fell asleep. Klara saw, in a dream, a big field that looked as blue as the sky, it was so thickly studded with bluebells, and Heidi heard the robber-bird up in the air screaming:

"Come! Come! Come!"

Chapter 8

SOMETHING UNEXPECTED HAPPENS

~~~~~~

VERY EARLY the next morning the uncle came out of the hut and looked around to see what kind of a day it was going to be.

On the lofty mountain peaks lay a reddish-golden light. A cool breeze was beginning to rock the branches of the fir trees to and fro. The sun was coming up. First, the high mountain tops, then the green hills began to shine with golden light. Finally the dark shadows gently faded away in the valley, and both heights and depths gleamed in the sunshine.

The uncle brought the wheel chair out of the shop and placed it, ready for the journey, in front of the hut. Just as he went inside again to call the girls, Peter came climbing the mountain, looking angrier than ever.

For weeks the boy had not had Heidi to himself. When he came up in the morning, and when he went down again in the evening, she was usually talking to the strange girl in the wheel chair. Heidi had not visited the pasture all summer. Now at last she was coming, but with the stranger in the chair, and she would devote herself to Klara the whole time.

Peter knew how it would be, and this brought his secret anger to a climax. He looked at the chair as though it were an enemy that had done him a great wrong and was going to do him a still greater wrong today.

He looked around. Everything was still; not a person was to be seen. Then, in his anger, he rushed at the chair and pushed it with such force that it started rolling down the slope of the moun-

tain and, in a moment, had disappeared.

Frightened by what he had done, Peter rushed up the Alm as if he had wings. He did not stop once until he had reached a big blackberry bush behind which he could hide, for he was not anxious to have the uncle see him. From here he could look down the Alm, and what a sight met his eyes! His enemy had already gone rushing far below gaining speed as it traveled. It turned over and over again. It bounded up in the air and fell down on the ground once more, rolling over and over to its destruction.

Pieces of the chair were flying in every direction. Peter took such delight in the sight that he forgot to be afraid and jumped high in the air. He laughed aloud, he stamped with joy, he leaped around in circles. He was beside himself with delight, for without the chair the strange girl could not move about and would have to go away. Heidi would be alone and come up to the pasture again, and everything would be as it had been before. He did not stop to think what the consequences of his wicked deed might be.

When Heidi came out of the hut, she ran to the shop. Her grandfather followed with Klara in his arms.

"Where is the chair, Heidi? Did you roll it away?" he asked.

"No, grandfather," said Heidi, looking worried. "You said you left it standing by the door. Oh, do you suppose the wind has blown the chair down to Dörfli? If it has, by the time we get it back, it will be too late for us to go up on the Alm."

Meanwhile the wind had grown stronger. It rattled the shop door and suddenly threw it with a crash back against the wall.

"If the wind has blown the chair down the Alm, we can never get it back, for it has been broken into a hundred pieces by now," said the grandfather. He stepped around the corner of the hut and looked down the slopes. "But I don't see how that could have happened. I left the chair on the side of the hut where it would be protected from the wind."

"Oh, what a shame! We can't go now, and perhaps never," wailed Klara. "Now I shall have to go home, for I haven't any chair."

"We will go up to the pasture this time just as we planned," said the grandfather. "Then we shall see what will happen next. I wonder why Peter is so long coming this morning," he added to himself.

The children shouted for joy, and Heidi led Schwänli and Bärli out of the shed. The grandfather went back into the hut for extra shawls. Then carrying Klara with one arm and the shawls on the other, he started up the mountain.

"Forward, march!" he said. "The goats may come with us."

This pleased Heidi. With one arm around Schwänli's neck and the other around Bärli's, she followed her grandfather. When they reached the pasture, they were surprised to see the other goats peacefully grazing here and there on the slopes and Peter lying full length on the ground.

"Another time I will cure you of passing us by, sleepy-head. What did you mean?" the uncle called to him.

Peter jumped up at the sound of the well-known voice.

"Nobody was up," he replied.

"Did you see anything of the chair?" asked the uncle.

"Of what?" said Peter crossly.

The uncle said nothing more. He spread the shawls on the sunny slope, placed Klara on them, and asked if she was comfortable.

"Yes, thank you," said Klara. "As comfortable as in my chair. Oh, it is so beautiful here, so beautiful!"

"I must go back now," said the grandfather, "so just enjoy yourselves. Heidi, I left the dinner packed in the bag over in the shade. Peter will give you as much milk as you want to drink, but be sure that it comes from Schwänli. Good-by, for now. I am going down and see what has become of the chair."

The sky was deep blue, and not a cloud was to be seen anywhere. The snow field beyond them sparkled like thousands of gold and silver stars. The gray rocky peaks stood high and steadfast in their places, as they had done for ages, looking down solemnly into the valley. The mountain wind passed over the heights and blew softly around the sunny Alm.

The children were very happy. Now and then a little goat would come and lie down by them for a while. The affectionate

Schneehöpli came most frequently and laid her little head against Heidi, and would not have gone away at all if another one of the flock had not driven her off. Thus Klara learned to know the goats. After they grew used to her, they came quite near and rubbed their heads against her shoulder.

Several hours had passed in this way, when it occurred to Heidi that she would like to go up the mountain a little farther to the place where so many flowers grew. When her grandfather came back in the evening, he could carry Klara up there, but perhaps the flowers would have closed their eyes by then. Besides, Heidi had waited so long to see them that she felt she could wait no longer.

"Would you mind, Klara," she asked timidly, "if I leave you alone for a few minutes? I would like to see how the flowers are; but wait—"

She jumped up and pulled some fragrant bunches of green plants. Schneehöpli immediately came running toward her, and Heidi led the goat back to Klara.

"Schneehöpli will stay with you, so you won't be alone after all," said Heidi, tossing the leaves into Klara's lap. Then she ran away to take a good look at the flowers.

Klara was perfectly willing to stay alone with the goat. It was so tame that it nestled up to this new friend and ate the leaves slowly out of her fingers. Klara was delighted. She realized how wonderful it was to be able to help someone else and not always be obliged to take help from others. She wanted to do something to give pleasure to some person, as she was now pleasing Schneehöpli. She had never felt so happy as she threw her arms around the goat's neck and exclaimed:

"Oh, Schneehöpli, how beautiful it is up here! If I only could stay here with you always!"

Meanwhile Heidi had climbed farther up the mountain. Suddenly she squealed out loud with delight. The slope lay covered with the shining gold of bright rock roses. Thick clusters of blue-bells nodded above them. Little brown blossoms stretched up their round heads modestly here and there between the golden flower-cups and filled the air with a spicy fragrance.

Heidi drew in long breaths of sweet air, and then turned around and came panting with excitement back to Klara.

"Oh, you really must come," she called. "Everything is so beautiful, and perhaps by evening the flowers won't be so lovely. Perhaps I can carry you; don't you think I could?"

Klara looked at the excited Heidi in surprise. "What are you thinking about? You are ever so much smaller than I. If I only could walk!"

Heidi looked around, trying to think of some new plan. Up on the higher slopes she could see Peter sitting, staring down at them. He had been sitting there for hours always gazing down as though he could not realize what he saw. He had destroyed the hated chair so the stranger would not be able to move about. Yet there she was sitting before him on the ground next to Heidi. It could not be possible; yet it was true.

Heidi looked up at him. "Come down here, Peter!" she called.

"Won't," he called back.

"But you must! Come, I can't do it alone, and you must help me."

"Won't," he said again.

Heidi ran a little way up the mountain toward him. She stood there with flashing eyes. "Peter, if you don't come at once, I will do something to you that you won't like at all."

Peter began to tremble. At first he had been much pleased with himself, but when Heidi spoke as though she knew all about what he had done, he was afraid she might tell her grandfather. Peter did not know what would happen if the Alm-Uncle learned the truth about the chair. His distress almost choked him as he rose and hurried toward Heidi.

"I am coming, but please don't do it," he begged, so frightened that Heidi was touched.

"All right," she said assuringly, "only come with me. There is nothing to be afraid of in what I want you to do."

When they reached Klara, Heidi began to give orders. Peter was to take Klara firmly under one arm and Heidi was to take her under the other. But though the children succeeded in lifting Klara to her feet, she found it hard to stand.

"You must put your arm around my neck now very firmly," said Heidi. "Now you must take Peter's arm also, and lean on it very hard. Then we can carry you."

Peter had never given anyone his arm before. When Klara tried to take it, he held it down stiffly by his side like a long stick.

"That is not the way to do," said Heidi. "You must make a ring of your arm, so Klara can put hers through it. She must lean on it very hard so we can move along."

This was done, but the children did not make much progress. Klara was not light, and Heidi was so much shorter than Peter that she did not have equal support on both sides. Klara tried to bear weight on her feet a little, but she could not move them forward.

"Just stamp right down," suggested Heidi. "Then it will hurt you less afterwards."

"Do you think so?" said Klara doubtfully.

However she obeyed. She tried to take one firm step on the ground and then another, though each time she cried out in pain. Then she lifted one foot again and put it down more carefully.

"Why, that didn't hurt nearly so much," she said, delighted.

"Do it once more," urged Heidi.

Klara did so, and then again and again she took a step, and

suddenly she cried out excitedly:

"I can do it, Heidi! Oh, I can! See! I can take steps, one after another."

"Why, you can walk," Heidi shouted. "If only Grandfather would come! Now you can walk, now you can really walk!"

Leaning on Heidi and Peter, Klara tried again, and with each step she gained more confidence.

Heidi was beside herself with delight.

"Now, we can come up to the pasture together every day. We can go wherever we please on the mountain! You can go about as

I do all the rest of your life, and never be pushed in a chair. It's the most wonderful thing that could happen!"

Klara agreed with all her heart. Surely she could have no greater fortune in the world than to be well and be able to go about like other people.

It was not far to the slope where the flowers grew. Already the children could see the gleam of the golden roses in the sun. Then they came to the clusters of bluebells where the sunny ground showed through invitingly.

"Can't we sit down here?" asked Klara who had never sat on the ground before.

This was just what Heidi wished to do, and the children sat down in the midst of the flowers. All around them were the nodding bluebells, the shining golden roses, the red centauries, and everywhere the sweet fragrance of the brown blossoms and the spicy wild plum. Everything was so lovely—so lovely!

As Heidi sat beside her friend, it suddenly occurred to her that at last Klara had been made well and that this was even more wonderful than all the beauty around them. Klara was silent, hardly able to realize her good fortune. The sunshine and the fragrance of flowers overpowered her with such a feeling of joy that she could not speak.

Peter lay silent also, for he was almost asleep. The wind blew softly behind the protecting rocks and whispered among the bushes. Now and then Heidi had to get up and run about, for there was always some place still more beautiful to explore.

Suddenly Peter awoke. He had to rub his eyes hard, for he had been dreaming that the wheel chair was standing again, all upholstered in red and unharmed, in front of the hut. Then his distress, which had disappeared in his dream, came back to him. Although Heidi had promised not to do anything, he was afraid that his wicked deed would be found out. So he was very meek and willing to do everything as Heidi wished.

When the three children came back to the pasture, Heidi brought out the well-filled dinner bag. She had noticed that morning what good things her grandfather had put into it, and she had known how pleased Peter would be. But when he had acted so disagreeably, she had wanted to make him understand that he could not have his share unless he behaved. That was why she had threatened to do something that he would not like.

But as she spread the dinner on the ground before them, she gave the biggest helping of all to Peter. He ate silently without stopping until he had finished every crumb. But he did not enjoy his meal as much as he had expected. Something lay in his stomach which gnawed and choked him at every mouthful.

The children had returned so late to their dinner that they had scarcely finished when the grandfather was seen coming up the Alm to get them. Heidi rushed to meet him. She was so excited that she could hardly find words to tell him what had happened. But he understood at once, and his face lighted up with joy. He hastened his steps, and when he reached Klara, he said, smiling:

"So you ventured and you have succeeded!"

He helped Klara up, put his left arm around her, and held out his right arm as a support for her hand. In this way she walked more easily than before. But after she had taken several steps, he took her up in his arms.

"We must not overdo it," he said. "It is time to go home now, for you need rest."

When Peter reached Dörfli that evening, he saw a crowd of people pushing each other this way and that. He was curious to know what they were looking at and elbowed his way through.

Then he saw what it was.

On the grass lay the middle part of the wheel chair with a portion of the back still hanging to it. The red upholstery and the bright nails still showed how splendid it had once looked.

"I was here when it came down," said the baker, who was standing next to Peter. "It was worth at least five hundred francs. I wonder how it happened."

"The wind must have brought it down; the uncle said so himself," remarked Barbel.

"I hope so," said the baker doubtfully. "If any person is responsible, he will be in a fine fix. If the gentleman in Frankfurt hears of it, he will try to find out how it happened. As for me, I am glad that I haven't been on the Alm for two years. Suspicion may fall on anyone who was seen up there at that time."

Peter had heard enough. He crept meekly out of the crowd and ran up the mountain as if someone were after him. The baker's words had given him a terrible scare. He felt sure that at any moment an officer from Frankfurt might come to look into the matter, and find out who had pushed the chair down the mountain. Then Peter would be seized and sent to the house of correction in Frankfurt. His hair seemed to stand on end from fear at the thought.

By the time he reached home, he was much distressed. He refused to talk to anyone, and he would not eat his potatoes. He crept hurriedly into bed and groaned.

"Peterli must have been eating sorrel again," said his mother. "That is what makes him groan so."

"You must give him a little more bread to take with him. Give him a piece of mine tomorrow," said the grandmother compassionately.

That night when Heidi and Klara looked up from their beds at the starlight, Heidi said:

"Haven't you been thinking all day how good it is that the dear Lord doesn't give us what we pray so hard for, when he knows of something much better?"

"What do you mean, Heidi?" asked Klara.

"Don't you remember how hard I prayed in Frankfurt that I might go home right away? When I couldn't go, I thought the dear Lord had not heard me. But, do you know, if I had gone right away, you would never have come up on the mountain, and you wouldn't have got well."

"Perhaps we should not pray at all," said Klara, "because the dear Lord always has something better in mind than we know to ask him for."

"Oh, Klara," said Heidi, "we ought to pray to the dear Lord every day. Then he will know that we do not forget that we receive everything from him. If we do not receive what we would like, we must not think the dear Lord has not listened, and stop praying, but we must pray like this: 'Now I know, dear Lord, that you have something better in store, and I will be glad that you will be so good to me.'"

"How did you find out all this, Heidi?" asked Klara.

"Your grandmamma explained it to me first, and then it happened exactly so. I think we ought really to thank the dear Lord heartily tonight, because you are able to walk now."

"Yes, indeed, Heidi; you are right, and I am glad that you reminded me. I was so happy I almost forgot it."

Then the children prayed, and each thanked the dear Lord in her own way for sending such a wonderful blessing to Klara, who had been ill so long.

The next morning the grandfather suggested that they write the grandmamma to come up on the Alm at once. But the children had another plan. They wanted to surprise her. First, Klara was to learn to walk better so that she could go a little way with only Heidi's support, but the grandmamma must not have the least suspicion of this beforehand. The grandfather thought that Klara would be ready in a week, and it was decided to ask the grandmamma to pay them a visit at the end of that time.

The days which followed were the most wonderful Klara had passed on the Alm. Every morning she awoke with this thought:

"I am well! I am well! I do not need to sit in a wheel chair any longer. I can go about by myself like other people!"

Then she practiced walking. Every day she found it easier, and she took longer walks. The exercise gave her such an appetite that the grandfather made her slices of bread and butter thicker and larger than before, and he was well pleased to see them disappear. He filled bowl after bowl with foaming milk for Klara to drink.

The end of the week finally came, and with it the day that was to bring the grandmamma back to the Alm.

Chapter 9

PARTING TO MEET AGAIN

A DAY BEFORE her arrival, the grandmamma had written a letter telling exactly when she was coming. Peter brought this letter with him early the next morning on his way to the pasture. He handed it to the uncle who stood outside the hut with the children; then he rushed off as if something had frightened him. After stopping only once to look behind him, he gave a leap and ran up the mountain.

"Grandfather," said Heidi, "why does Peter act as big Türk does when he feels the rod behind him?"

"Perhaps Peter feels that there is a rod behind him too, and knows he deserves it," answered her grandfather.

Peter ran without stopping until he could no longer be seen from below. Only then did he dare stand still, turning his head timidly in every direction. Suddenly he leaped into the air and looked behind him, as frightened as if someone had just seized him by the nape of the neck. From behind every bush and out of every thicket, he thought he saw a policeman from Frankfurt rushing out at him.

Meanwhile Heidi had gone into the hut to put it in order, for she wanted everything to look tidy for the grandmamma. She cleaned in every corner, while Klara watched, and they chattered so merrily that the morning passed before they realized it. Then they came out and sat down on the bench in front of the hut to wait. At this moment the grandfather returned from a walk, carrying a bunch of deep-blue gentians. They were so

217

lovely that the children shouted for joy.

They settled down to wait again. But every little while Heidi jumped up and looked down the mountain, hoping to catch sight of the grandmamma's party. At last she saw exactly what she had been expecting. First, came the guide, and then the grandmamma on a white horse. Last of all, came the porter with a big basket on his back, for the grandmamma would never think of coming up on the mountain without taking plenty of wraps with her.

Nearer and nearer they came. When they reached the hut, the grandmamma looked down at the children from her horse.

"What do I see, Klärchen? You are not sitting in your chair!" she exclaimed in alarm and dismounted hastily. But before she had reached the children, she clapped her hands and exclaimed in the greatest excitement:

"Klärchen, is it you or is it not? You have red cheeks as round as apples! Child! I don't know you any longer!"

She was about to rush at Klara, when Heidi slipped unnoticed from the bench. Klara stood up, and, leaning on her friend's shoulder, calmly started to walk. The grandmamma stood still, frozen with fear, for her only thought was that Heidi was trying to do something rash.

But what did she see before her!

Klara was walking upright and safely beside Heidi. The girls looked at her with beaming faces. She rushed toward them. Laughing and crying, she embraced Klara, then Heidi, then Klara again. In her delight she could find no words.

Suddenly she caught sight of the uncle, who was standing by the bench and smiling with satisfaction.

"My dear uncle! We have you to thank for this," she said. "It is your care and nursing—"

"And our Lord's sunshine and mountain air," interrupted the

uncle, smilingly.

"Yes, and Schwänli's milk, too," added Klara. "Grandmamma, you ought to know how I can drink the goat's milk, and how good it is!"

"I can see that by your cheeks, Klärchen," said her grandmamma, laughing. "I cannot look at you enough! I must send a telegram to your father in Paris; he must come immediately. I will not tell him why; this will be the greatest joy of his life. My dear uncle, can the men take a telegram down the mountain for us?"

"They have gone," he replied, "but if the grandmamma is in haste, we can send the goatherd."

The uncle went a little way aside and gave such a penetrating whistle through his fingers that the echo whistled back from the rocks above. It was not long before Peter came running down, for he knew the whistle well. He was white as chalk, for he thought the Alm-Uncle was calling him to judgment. But the Alm-Uncle only handed him a paper on which the grandmamma had written a few words, and told him to take it to the post-master in Dörfli.

So Peter went along, with the paper in his hand, much relieved for this time.

At last the others were able to sit down quietly together around the table in front of the hut. The grandmamma had to be told everything from the beginning: how at first the grandfather had tried to have Klara stand and then take steps, how they had taken the journey up to the pasture and the wind had rolled away the chair; how Klara's eagerness to see the flowers had brought about her first attempt to walk. It was a long time before the children finished their story, for every little while the grandmamma interrupted:

"Is it really possible? Is the little girl before me, with the round, fresh face, my pale, weak Klärchen?"

Meanwhile Herr Sesemann had finished his business in Paris and was also preparing a surprise. Without writing a word to his mother, he took the train one sunny morning for Basle. He had been separated from his little daughter for weeks, and he had been seized with such a longing to see her that he felt he could not wait another day.

He reached Ragatz a few hours after his mother had left there. When he found that she had returned to the Alm, he immediately hired a carriage and drove to Mayenfeld. From here he drove to Dörfli and then he began the long walk up the mountain.

But the climb proved harder and more tiresome than he had expected, and when no hut appeared in sight he was worried. He had been told that the goatherd Peter lived in a hut halfway up the Alm, and when he looked at the footpaths leading in all directions, he was afraid he might have taken the wrong one. Or perhaps the hut lay on the other side of the mountain.

Herr Sesemann stopped and looked around, but there was no human being of whom he could ask the way. Far and wide there was nothing to be seen, nothing to be heard. Only the flies buzzed in the sunshine, and a merry bird piped here and there on a lonely larch tree.

Just then someone came running down from above; it was Peter with the dispatch in his hand. He was running straight ahead, down the steep places, and as soon as he came close enough, Herr Sesemann beckoned. Peter came, trembling and frightened, not straightforward but sideways, as if he could only advance with one foot and had to drag the other after him.

"Here, youngster, brace up!" said Herr Sesemann encouragingly. "Tell me if this path will bring me up to the hut, where the old man lives with the child Heidi. Some people from Frankfurt are visiting there."

Peter gasped in terror. Then he darted away and, in his haste, fell head over heels, down the steep mountainside. Over and over he rolled, turning almost as many somersaults as the wheel chair had turned, but fortunately he did not go to pieces as the chair had done. Finally, on the last high slope above Dörfli, he rolled against a bush to which he could cling.

"What a bashful mountaineer," said Herr Sesemann to himself as he continued his journey, "to be so afraid of a stranger!"

Peter lay trembling with fear trying to think what had happened to him. He felt stiff and sore from his fall. He was terrified at the thought of the stranger who had asked the way to the Alm-Uncle's hut, for Peter was convinced that a policeman from Frankfurt had come for him at last.

"Well, well, what's this?" said a voice close by, and Peter looked up to see the baker grinning down at him. "You must have come down in quite a hurry!"

Peter jumped to his feet. New fear seized him; the baker must know that the chair had been pushed. Without looking back once, he ran up the mountain again.

He would have preferred to go home and creep into his bed so that no one could find him. But the uncle had told him to come back soon so the flock would not be left alone too long. In the course of his fall he had lost the telegram which he was supposed to give the postmaster in Dörfli. So he started back up the Alm, limping and groaning and hoping that no one would see him.

Meanwhile Herr Sesemann had reached the goatherd's hut, and knew then that he was on the right path. He climbed with renewed zeal, and at last he saw his goal before him. There stood the Alm hut and the dark branches of the old fir trees swaying above it. He smiled, thinking he was soon to surprise his child.

But a greater surprise, one he little suspected, was in store for him. When the company in front of the hut saw him coming, a tall young girl with yellow hair and rosy cheeks arose from the bench. She leaned on Heidi whose dark eyes were sparkling with excitement, and walked toward him with slow but steady steps.

Herr Sesemann stopped short. Exactly so had Klara's mother looked. Tears fell from his eyes, he gazed at the approaching children. He did not know whether he was awake or dreaming.

"Papa, don't you know me?" Klara called. "Am I so changed?"
The father rushed forward and took her in his arms.

"Yes, you are changed! Is it you, Klärchen, is it really you?"
he exclaimed. Then he stepped back and looked at her again to
see whether it really was Klara standing erect before him.

Then the grandmamma came out, for she could not wait any
longer to see her son's happy face.

"Well, my dear son, what do you say now?" said the grandmamma. "The surprise which you have given us is very lovely,
but the one prepared for you is still lovelier, is it not? But now
you must meet the uncle, our greatest benefactor."

"Certainly, and I must greet Heidi, too," said Herr Sesemann,
shaking hands with the child. "Well? But I don't need to ask;
no Alpine rose could be more blooming. This is a great joy to
me, child."

Heidi looked with beaming eyes at the kind Herr Sesemann.
Then the grandmamma took him to the Alm-Uncle. While the
two men were shaking hands and Herr Sesemann was trying
to express his deep-felt thanks, the grandmamma decided she
wanted to look at the old fir trees again.

Here there was another surprise awaiting her. Under the fir
trees, where the long branches had left a free space, there was
a big bunch of deep-blue gentians, as fresh and shining as if
they had grown there.

The grandmamma clapped her hands with delight, and called
the children.

"How lovely!" she said. "Heidi, did you put these here to
surprise me?"

"No," said Heidi, "but I know who did."

"There are ever so many more up in the pasture," said Klara.
"Guess who brought the flowers for you early this morning."

At that moment a gentle rustling was heard behind the fir

trees. Peter had come back, but when he saw who was standing in front of the hut with the uncle he had decided to take the long way around to the pasture. But just as he was trying to slip past, behind the fir trees, the grandmamma caught sight of him. She thought that perhaps Peter had brought the flowers, and that he was trying to creep away because he was so timid and modest.

"Come, my lad," she called, "don't be afraid."

Petrified with fear, Peter stood still. "Now they've found out," he thought. He was very pale as he stepped out from behind the fir trees.

"Come right straight here," said the grandmamma encouragingly. "Now tell me, my boy, if you did this."

Peter did not lift his eyes so did not see where the grandmamma's finger was pointing. He had noticed the uncle standing by the corner of the hut, watching him out of keen gray eyes. Next to the uncle stood the most terrible person Peter could think of—the man he supposed was a policeman from Frankfurt.

"Y-Y-Yes," he stammered, trembling in every limb as he answered the grandmamma's question.

"There now," she said, "what is there to be frightened about?"

"Because—because—because it is broken to pieces and can never be made whole again." Peter brought these words out with difficulty, and his knees shook so he could hardly stand.

The grandmamma walked over to the corner of the hut. "My dear uncle, is the poor boy out of his mind?" she asked.

"Not in the least," said the uncle. "But the boy is the wind that blew away the wheel chair, and now he is expecting the punishment that he deserves."

The grandmamma could not believe this, for she did not think Peter looked wicked. Besides he had no reason to destroy the wheel chair which was so much needed. But the uncle had been

suspicious all along, and he told the grandmamma what he thought must have happened.

When he had finished, the lady burst out in great excitement, "We must not punish the poor fellow any further. Let us be just. Strange people came here and took away Heidi, his only friend. Anger drove him to take revenge, and in anger we all are foolish."

The grandmamma went back to the bench under the fir trees and called Peter to her.

"Stop trembling, my boy, and listen to me," she said kindly. "You sent the wheel chair down the mountain in order to smash it. That was a wicked deed, and you knew it very well. You also knew that you deserved to be punished, and you have tried very hard not to let anyone know what you did. But you see whoever does a wicked thing and thinks no one knows about it is mistaken. The dear Lord sees and hears everything, and as soon as he notices that a person wants to conceal his wicked deed, he quickly awakens a little watchman that sleeps in each one of us. This little watchman has a goad with which he pricks the person who has done wrong, saying, 'You are going to be found out! You are going to be punished!' Is that not true, Peter?"

Peter nodded penitently.

"Furthermore, in this case you were disappointed," the grandmamma continued. "The wrong you did helped the one you wished to harm. Klara no longer had a chair to be carried in, and when she wanted to see the flowers she made a great effort to walk. So she learned how, and now she keeps on improving. After a while she will be able to go up to the pasture every day. Do you understand, Peter? When one wishes to do a wicked thing, the dear Lord can take it quickly into his own hands and turn it into good for the one who was to be harmed. The scoundrel has his trouble for nothing and injures himself.

"Remember that, Peter, and if you ever want to do anything wicked, think of the little watchman inside you. Will you do that?"

"Yes, I will," answered Peter, very much impressed and casting another anxious glance at the man he thought was a policeman.

"That is good; then the matter is settled," said the grandmamma. "But now you ought to have something you like to remember the people from Frankfurt by. Tell me, my boy, what would you like to have best?"

Peter lifted his head and stared at the grandmamma with his round, astonished eyes. He had been expecting some frightful punishment, and now he was to have whatever he liked best.

"Yes, I mean it," said the grandmamma. "You shall have something you like as a token that we will think no more about the wrong you did."

It began to dawn on Peter that he had no punishment to fear, and that the good lady had rescued him from the power of the policeman. He felt as relieved as if a mountain which was almost crushing him had been taken away. He also realized that it was better to confess his faults.

"I lost the paper, too," he said.

The grandmamma had to think a little while before she realized that he was talking about the telegram.

"There, that is right to tell me about it," she said kindly. "Always confess, if you have done wrong. Now what would you like to have?"

The thought that he could choose anything in the world made Peter dizzy. The whole fair at Mayenfeld came before his eyes, with all the beautiful things upon which he had often gazed for hours and had thought he could never have. Peter had never owned more than five pfennigs, and the lovely red whistles and round-handled knives and other alluring objects had always cost twice that much.

He stood, deep in thought, trying to decide if he would rather have a knife or a whistle. Then a bright idea came to him: if he asked for money he would not have to decide until the next fair.

"Ten pfennigs," he replied.

"That is not extravagant," the grandmamma said with a smile. "Come here."

She opened her purse and took out a big, round, silver coin. On it she laid two small ten-pfennig pieces.

"This big coin is worth nearly as many ten-pfennig pieces as there are weeks in the year. You can use one every Sunday the whole year through."

"All my life long?" asked Peter innocently.

The grandmamma laughed so hard that the gentlemen stopped talking to hear what was going on.

The grandmamma kept on laughing.

"You shall have it, my boy; I will put it in my will. Then it will be handed over to you thus: To goatherd Peter a ten-pfennig piece weekly, as long as he lives."

Herr Sesemann nodded in assent and laughed too.

Peter looked again at the present in his hand, to see if it was really true. "Thank God!" he said.

Then he ran away, making extraordinary leaps. But this time he stayed on his feet, for now he was not driven by fear but by such happiness as he had never known before.

Later when in front of the Alm hut, they had ended their happy midday meal Klara took her father's hand.

"Oh, papa," she said, "if you only knew all that the grandfather has done for me! I shall never forget it. I wish I could do something to make him even half as happy as he has made me."

"That is my greatest desire also, my dear," said her father. "I have been wondering how we can prove our gratitude."

Herr Sesemann rose and went to the uncle, who was sitting beside the grandmamma.

"My dear friend, let us have a word together," he said, holding out his hand. "For years I have had no real happiness, for what good was my money when I could not make my child well and strong? But you, with the help of God, have made her well for me. I can never repay you for what you have done, but whatever is in my power I want to do. Tell me, how can I show my gratitude?"

The uncle watched the happy father with a smile of contentment.

"Herr Sesemann, I have had my share of joy in Klara's recovery," he said. "My pains have been well rewarded. I thank you for your kind offer, but there is nothing I need. As long as I live, I have enough for the child and myself. But I have one wish, and if that could be granted I would never have another worry."

"Name your wish, my friend!" urged Herr Sesemann.

"I am old," continued the uncle, "and cannot live much longer. When I go, I cannot leave the child anything, and she has no relatives, except one who might take advantage of her. If Herr Sesemann would assure me that Heidi need never go among strangers to seek her bread, then he would have richly rewarded me for what I have done for him and his child."

"But, my dear friend, that goes without saying," Herr Sesemann burst forth. "The child belongs to us. Ask my mother, my daughter; Heidi will never be left to other people! But if it will be any comfort to you, my friend, here is my hand on it. I will say even more. This child is not made for a life in a strange land. We have seen that. But she has made friends. The doctor is coming up here again this autumn, and will settle in this region. He found more pleasure in your company and the child's than in anyone else's. So, you see, Heidi will have two protectors. May you both be preserved to her for a long, long time!"

"The dear Lord grant it may be so!" the grandmamma added. Then she put her arm around Heidi and drew the child close.

"We must ask you a question also," she said. "Come, tell me: have you a wish you would like to have granted?"

"Indeed, I have," answered Heidi.

"Then speak right out," said the grandmamma. "What would you like to have, child?"

"I would like to get my bed in Frankfurt, with the three thick pillows and the thick quilt and give it to the grandmother. Then she would not have to lie with her head downhill so that she can hardly breathe. She would be warm enough under the quilt, and wouldn't always have to go to bed with a shawl on, because she is so terribly cold."

Heidi said this all in one breath in her eagerness.

"My dear Heidi," said the grandmamma, "it is a good thing that you remind me. In our joy we easily forget what we ought to think of most. When the dear Lord sends us something good, we ought to think of those who are in need! We will telegraph to Frankfurt! Rottenmeier shall have the bed packed up this very day and in two days more it will be here. God willing, the grandmother shall sleep well in it!"

Heidi danced merrily around the grandmamma. But all at once she stood still.

"I must go down and tell the grandmother as fast as I can," she said. "She will be troubled because I haven't been there for so long."

"No, no, Heidi! What are you thinking about?" said her grandfather reprovingly. "When one has visitors, one doesn't run away from them."

But the grandmamma took Heidi's part.

"My dear uncle, the child is right," she said. "We have taken her away from the poor grandmother for a long time.

"We shall all go together to see her. I shall wait for my horse there, then go on my way. We can send a telegram at once to Frankfurt from Dörfli. My son, what do you think of it?"

Herr Sesemann had not had a chance to speak about his plans. So he asked his mother to wait for a few minutes while he explained. Now that Klara was so much better he wanted to take her and the grandmamma on a little journey through Switzerland. He planned to spend the night in Dörfli and come back the next morning for Klara. They would meet the grandmamma in Ragatz and go on from there.

Klara was disappointed to hear that she must leave the Alm, but there were many other things for her to be happy about. Besides there was no time to give way to grief.

The grandmamma grasped Heidi's hand and led the way down the mountain to the grandmother's hut. The uncle picked Klara up in his arms and followed. Last of all came Herr Sesemann.

As Heidi walked beside Frau Sesemann, she talked about the grandmother: how she lived and how hard it was for her to get along, especially in winter. The grandmamma listened thoughtfully while Heidi told how the grandmother sat bowed over in her corner and trembled with the cold.

When they reached the hut, Brigitte was just hanging Peter's extra shirt out in the sun. She rushed into the house.

"They are all going away now, mother," she said. "There is a whole procession of them. The uncle is with them; he is carrying the sick child."

"Oh, must it really be?" sighed the grandmother. "Did you see whether they were taking Heidi with them? If I could only hear her voice once more!"

The door was suddenly flung open as if by a whirlwind. Heidi rushed up to the grandmother and threw her arms around her neck.

"Grandmother! Grandmother! My bed is coming from Frankfurt, with three pillows, and the thick quilt, too. In two days it will be here; the grandmamma said so."

Heidi talked fast, because she could hardly wait to see how happy the good news would make the grandmother. But though the grandmother smiled, there was sadness in her voice as she replied:

"Oh, what a good lady she is! I ought to be glad that she is going to take you with her, Heidi, but I shall not survive it long."

"Do not worry," said a friendly voice, and the grandmamma came forward to grasp the old lady's hand. "Heidi is going to stay here and make you happy. We shall want to see the child again, but we will come to her. We shall come up to the Alm every year, for we have reason to offer thanks to the dear Lord in this place where such a miracle has been wrought for *our* child."

There was a joyful light in the grandmother's face as she pressed Frau Sesemann's hand. "How is it possible that there are such good people who trouble themselves about a poor old woman and do so much for her?" she said.

"My good grandmother," answered Frau Sesemann, "before our Father in heaven we all are equally poor, and it is necessary to all of us that he should not forget us. And now we must leave you, but we hope to see you again when we come back next year to the Alm."

The next morning when Klara's father came for her, she shed a few tears because she had to leave the beautiful Alm.

"It will be summer again in no time," said Heidi, trying to comfort her friend. "When you come back, it will be more beautiful than ever. By then you'll be so strong you can walk all the time, and we can go up to the pasture with the goats every day and see the flowers."

Heidi's words comforted her a little.

"I will leave a greeting for Peter," Klara said, "and for all the goats, especially Schwänli. If only I could give Schwänli a present! She has helped so much to make me well."

"You might send her a little salt," suggested Heidi. "You know how she likes to lick the salt from grandfather's hand at night."

"Then I will send her a hundred pounds of salt from Frankfurt!" said Klara.

Herr Sesemann beckoned to the children, for he wished to start. Klara rode down the mountain on the grandmamma's white horse. Heidi stood at the edge of the slope and waved her hand to Klara until rider and horse disappeared in the distance.

The bed came from Frankfurt, and the grandmother still sleeps so well in it that she is gaining strength.

The kind grandmamma did not forget the hard winter on the mountain. She had a big box sent to goatherd Peter's house. There were so many warm shawls and blankets packed in it, in which the grandmother could wrap herself up, that she never has to sit in the corner shivering with cold.

The doctor is living in Dörfli now. On the advice of his friend, he purchased the old building where the uncle lived with Heidi in the winter, and which had once been a great mansion. The doctor is having the lofty room with the handsome stove rebuilt for his own dwelling. The other side is being restored as winter quarters for the uncle and Heidi, for the doctor knew the old man was independent and would want to have his own house. Behind it is a firmly built, warm goatshed where Schwänli and Bärli can spend the winter days in comfort.

The doctor and the Alm-Uncle are becoming better friends

every day, and when they climb about the building to look after the progress of the work, they talk of Heidi. To both of them their chief joy in the house is that they will be together with their happy child.

"My dear uncle," said the doctor one day, "I feel as if, next to you, I am the one to whom she belongs, and I want her to share in my property like my own child. So when we have to leave her, we shall know that she will be well provided for."

The uncle pressed the doctor's hand for a long time; he spoke not a word, but his good friend could read the old man's gratitude in his eyes.

Meanwhile Heidi and Peter were sitting with the grandmother, and Heidi had so much to tell them that she hardly stopped long enough to get her breath. All three were very happy because of the wonderful things that had happened. But Peter's mother, Brigitte, looked almost the happiest of all. Heidi had told her it was really true that Peter was to have a ten-pfennig piece every week for the rest of his life.

Finally the grandmother said:

"Heidi, read me a song of praise and thanksgiving! I feel like praising and glorifying our Lord in heaven and giving Him thanks for all that he has done for us."